Amber Stars

Amber Stars

Isabel Hansen

❄   I   ❄

SOMETIME AROUND THE ten-year mark of our friendship, Kiara stopped greeting me at her front door when I came over. Instead, she told me to just walk inside. At first, it felt weird but by the summer after my first year of university rolled around, I was well used to it.

Kiara told me to meet her in the backyard so I could have gone around the house, but I wanted to go through the air conditioning, even if it was only briefly. I had ridden my bike from my house to Kiara's since I still couldn't drive, and I wanted nothing more than to cool off.

"Hi, Mrs. Nichols," I said as I passed through the kitchen.

"Harlee, I've told you, call me Mary!" She said. She didn't even look up from where she was cutting vegetables at the kitchen island.

"Of course, Mary," I said as I stepped out onto the patio. Kiara was sitting on the edge of the pool at the far end of the yard. Like her mother, she didn't bother to acknowledge my existence when I walked outside, too entranced by something on her phone. I dropped my towel on the ground and slipped out of my clothes. I was wearing my bathing suit underneath, so I dove straight into the water. I swam under the surface until I reached Kiara.

"Hey," she said as I leaned against her leg.

"What are you looking at?" I asked. I couldn't see her phone screen from the angle I was standing at.

"Nothing," she sighed. She threw her phone onto her towel behind her then slipped into the water beside me. "How are you?"

"Fine. You?"

"Same," she said. Kiara and I rarely ran out of things to talk about, but we had just gotten back from a three-week road trip the day before, and I think it was safe to say we were both a little drained. "I'm cold. Want to go in the hot tub?"

She began swimming across the pool before I had the chance to respond. To be honest, I was still a little hot and found the pool water refreshing, but I got out after her anyway. I suppose I could have stayed in the pool alone, but that just wasn't what Kiara and I liked to do.

Before I got in the hot tub, I glanced at my phone quickly. I frowned at the new email notification on my home screen and went to open it.

"I have an email from my new boss," I said. I was starting a new job at a bookstore in a couple weeks, so I assumed it had something to do with training or the shift schedule.

"What does it say?" Kiara asked. I scanned it quickly.

"She's wondering if I can start work a little earlier than I was originally supposed to," I said. "Apparently, they're a little short-staffed."

"Oh," Kiara said. "Are you going to do it?"

"I don't know," I said. I put my phone back in my bag. "I'll respond later."

Of course, the money would be nice, but it would also mean having less time to spend with Kiara before she left for camp in two weeks. I was used to her leaving for the summers, but I always missed her a lot when she was gone, and I wanted to spend as much time with her as I could before she left.

"Don't say no on my account," Kiara said. I sat next to her in the hot tub.

"Who said I was?" I asked neutrally.

She shrugged. "I thought that might be why you're hesitating."

"You think very highly of yourself."

She was right, of course. But she didn't need to know that.

"I'm just saying, I have to prepare for work for the next couple of weeks," she said. "So I could do it while you're working, then we can do whatever we want while we hang out. And you'll have extra spending money."

"If I didn't know any better, I would say you're trying to get rid of me," I said.

Kiara gasped dramatically. "Moi? I would never."

"Mh-hm."

Still, her reasoning made sense. It wasn't like we

needed to spend every moment of our lives together, and it was only logical that I make some money while she had to be packing anyway.

I wiped my hand on my towel and quickly typed out an email saying that I would be happy to start work on Monday. Then, I threw my phone back in my bag and resolved to put the whole matter of working out of my mind so I could enjoy my last weekend of freedom.

$$\text{❈} \quad 2 \quad \text{❈}$$

THE AGE DIFFERENCE between my brothers and me shocked people whenever I told them, but it had always been normal to me. The older of two, Greyson, was ten years old and the younger one, Emery, was six years old, giving us a fourteen-year age gap. Since they were so young, they frequently had activities in the evenings that my parents took them to, leaving me the house to myself.

When I got home from Kiara's house, I found a note on the counter telling me that Greyson was at a birthday party and Emery had a soccer game that my parents were watching, so I was alone for dinner. That was pretty typical. I felt a twinge of regret for not staying at Kiara's house after her mother offered so many times because I wasn't really in the mood to cook, but I shook it off quickly. To the surprise of many of my friends, I was a pretty introverted person, and I appreciated the peace and quiet of an empty house.

I quickly ordered a pizza then headed upstairs. My room was a mess. I hadn't unpacked from the road trip I had just gotten back from, instead opting to leave my duffle bag and clothes on the floor. Along with that, I'd done a big book haul just before I'd left, so there were books strewn all about the room. There was a mix of books sitting in boxes and in small piles on the floor. I usually liked to keep a very tidy room, so the mess was stressing me out. I figured the best time to clean was when nobody was home to complain, so I got to work.

First, I put on my summer playlist, which consisted of every genre of the sun. Then I tied up my hair and looked around, trying to prioritize what to do first. I wanted to try to put the books away, but I was worried I was going to get distracted partway through that task and begin reading a book that seemed particularly interesting, so it was better to start off with the more tedious task first — doing my laundry. Although I frequently complained about doing various household chores, I actually didn't mind them all that much when I could leave my music playing like I was. I sang and danced along as I quickly did my laundry then turned to sort my books.

To keep track of my extremely long To Be Read list, I tracked every book I owned on Goodreads. I would tag every book that I bought but hadn't read as a part of my 'Physical TBR' shelf on Goodreads. This made putting the books away a pretty tedious task, but I knew it would be well worth it.

I was just finishing this up when my phone started ringing, and Kiara's name flashed across the screen. I rolled my eyes but still smiled. I'd only been apart from her for a couple hours, and she was already calling me.

"Hey," I said when I answered.

"Hi, hi, hi!" Kiara said energetically. I could just imagine her jumping up and down.

"Did you have coffee with dinner or something?" I asked. "You sound like you're bouncing off the walls."

"No! Well, yes. Kinda."

"Kinda?" I asked, an amused smile on my lips.

"I had some coffee with Bailey's, and I thought it was decaf, but maybe it wasn't."

"Maybe," I said as if there was even an ounce of doubt. "What's up?"

"I—" She cut herself off. "I already forgot."

I frowned. "You called me less than a minute ago, and you already forgot why?"

"Yep!" I would have assumed she would be upset or confused by that fact, but she sounded downright chipper. "Anyway, what are you up to?"

"Just cleaning up my room," I said. "Putting away all the books I bought a couple weeks ago."

"Why didn't you wait to buy them until you started work?" Kiara asked. "You get an employee discount, don't you?"

"Yeah, but I didn't get these books from there," I said. "They're from an online bargain shop. Anyway, I finally put them all away and updated my Goodreads shelves."

"How many books do you have on your TBR now?" She asked, amused.

"Not that many!" I defended. I opened my laptop

to check and had to clear my throat before saying, "My physical TBR only has 324 books right now."

Kiara made a choking noise. "I'm sorry, did you say 324?"

"Yes..." I said. I was a little overwhelmed by the number. Maybe I needed to go on a book buying ban or something.

"How about your general TBR?" Kiara asked. "Is it like 500 or something?"

"Probably something like that," I said, but I went to check it. I was a little scared to see the number — anytime I heard about a book that sounded even somewhat interesting, I added it to my general TBR. My eyes widened when I saw the shelf number. "It's only, you know, a thousand books." I said the last part quietly as if that made it any better.

"A thousand?" Kiara screeched.

"Yeah, just 1,328," I said. "No big deal."

"Harlee, if you read a book every day, it would take you like four years to finish that entire list," Kiara said. "And by that point, you would have added so many more books that you'll never catch up."

I hadn't thought about it like that. I guess I had to accept that I would never finish my TBR, as much as I would like it.

"But," I said, "if I read a book a day, I would finish my physical TBR in a little less than a year."

"That does not make this better."

I sighed. "I know."

Besides, I knew reading a book was an impossible feat for me to manage. The vast majority of the books I read were at least 300 pages long, and while I loved reading, I could not read one of those every single day.

"My mom's yelling for me," Kiara sighed. "I'll call you later, okay?"

"Sure," I said. Chances were, she wouldn't call me back that night, and then we would meet up in person the next day, but I appreciated the sentiment all the same.

After we hung up, I threw my phone back on my bed and looked over my shelves. Kiara was right that the list would only keep growing as I found new books I wanted to read. I needed to make a dent in the pile somehow.

I turned back to my computer and looked for any reading challenges that might be running that summer. A couple of them looked fun, but none of them seemed like enough to help me finish up my pile. I sighed. Maybe I just needed to change my yearly reading goal. I already had a goal to read 100 books in the year, and I was easily following that — when I wasn't reading for fun, I was reading for my English degree — but increasing that goal was probably the only way to get this done.

I thought for a moment. As far as I knew, I had about nine weeks left of my summer vacation. If I wanted to read fifty books in the summer, I only had to read five to six books a week. An aggressive schedule, to be sure, but one that I was sure I could handle. Work did take up a good amount of my time, but with Kiara at camp all summer, I wouldn't have much else to do other than reading. I hopped off my bed and searched my bookshelves. Every week, I could pick out five books that I wanted to read and leave them out, so I could easily keep track.

I picked the five books from my recent book haul that I was the most excited about, then I laid on my bed and began reading. This challenge would be a breeze.

3

I GOT UP EARLY on Monday morning to get ready for work. I had already picked out my outfit the night before, a simple blouse and jeans, but I still had to do my hair and makeup the morning of. It wasn't like I needed to dress very nice to work at a bookstore, but I enjoyed fashion and makeup, and being put together made me feel less nervous.

I was working the morning shift, so as soon as I finished my morning coffee, I needed to bike over to the bookstore. The bike ride was long enough to make me wish that I had a car (and a driver's license), and all I could do was remind myself that I would be much more fit by the end of the summer because of this.

A blast of air conditioning hit me as I walked through the automatic doors that led inside the store. To my left was the checkout counter, and behind it was the bookstore manager, Tracy, who I'd met a few times before then when I was interviewing for the job.

"Hello, Harlee," Tracy said as soon as I walked in.

She walked around the counter, so she was on the same side as me.

"Tracy," I said with a slight nod. I felt a little underdressed for the job when I saw her dressed in a nice pantsuit with her braids pulled into a nice bun. Of course, I knew it made sense for us to be dressed differently since I was only a bookseller and she was the manager, but it still felt a little strange. I made sure to hold my head up and act like I thought everything was fine anyway.

"Why don't we step into the office for a moment," Tracy suggested. "We can go over what you'll be doing today."

"That sounds great," I said. She waved her dark hand in what I thought was a 'follow me' gesture and led me to the office on the far end of the store. I glanced around as we walked. Although the store wasn't open for another fifteen minutes, the few store employees were going about their jobs.

Tracy closed the door behind us when we went into her office and sat down in the swivel chair behind the desk, then gestured for me to sit in one of the chairs in front of it. She clasped her hands and placed them on the desk, and for a moment, I felt like I was in my high school principal's office again.

"How are you this morning?" She asked.

"I'm fantastic, thank you," I said. I was exhausted from being up so early, but I obviously wasn't going to say that.

She smiled genuinely. "That's great. I saw that you did all the online training modules, so you're ready to get started. Like I mentioned in your interview, you will have on-the-job training for the next couple of days. I assume you're still all right with that?"

"Yes, I am," I said. I wasn't sure why she asked anyway. I didn't exactly have another choice.

"Fantastic." She shifted some papers around. "I have your contract and direct deposit information here; that's perfect. You'll be paid every other Friday, starting next week."

There was a knock on the door behind me.

"Come in," Tracy called. The door creaked open. I didn't turn around to look, but I imagined someone peeking their head inside.

"You wanted to see me?" The person asked. The voice sounded familiar, but I couldn't quite put my finger on it.

"Ah, yes." Tracy stood up and walked around the desk. "Come in. I want you to meet our newest employee."

I stood up as well and turned. I opened my mouth to say hello but froze when I saw my new coworker.

"Harlee, this is Robyn," Tracy said, gesturing to the girl next to her. "Robyn, Harlee."

We didn't need introductions. It may have been five years since I'd last seen Robyn, but I would recognize her face anywhere. Her stupid fucking face that I wanted to punch. What the hell was she smiling like that for?

"It's nice to meet you," Robyn said.

"You too," I said. I wasn't sure why she was pretending she didn't know me, but I wouldn't be the first one to break.

"Robyn, I was thinking you could show Harlee the

ropes today," Tracy said. *Oh, hell no.* The fake smile was frozen on Robyn's face. I could almost see the gears turning in her mind, her trying to find a way to get out of this. I couldn't help but be a little satisfied at seeing her trapped like this, even if the outcome wouldn't be any better for me. She had always thought so highly of herself, and I loved seeing her knocked down a few pegs.

"I... think I was supposed to be on the floor today," Robyn said slowly. "I'm not sure that's the best way to train someone."

"It will be fine!" Tracy said brightly. "You're the only one here who has trained someone before, so this is best."

That stupid smile was still on Robyn's face, though it was looking more forced by the moment.

"Of course," she said.

"Why don't you two get started with that now?" Tracy suggested. Robyn stiffly turned and walked out. I wanted nothing more than to stay where I was, but I followed her. As soon as the door closed behind us, the smile dropped off Robyn's face, and she stormed off across the shop. Luckily, I was taller than her, so it wasn't much work to keep up.

"Of all the places you could work, you just had to work here?" Robyn snapped once we were near the front of the store, where nobody else would hear us.

"I could say the same to you," I said icily.

"I've worked here for more than three years now," she said. "And it was never a problem until you showed up."

"It's not like I got you fired or something," I said.

Under my breath, I added, "As much as I would like to."

I was surprised to hear that she had worked there for so long. I came to the store regularly, and I had never seen her around. It was improbable that she was never working when I came by, so my best guess was that she avoided me whenever I'd come in. I smirked at the thought.

"These are the cash registers," she said, throwing a lazy hand in their direction. "Do you know how to use them?"

"I've worked retail before if that's what you're asking," I said.

"Okay, they probably work the same as other stores," she said. She brushed past me to show me other areas of the store. Some training this was turning out to be.

The whole day continued as much of the same. Robyn showed me how to do inventory, stock shelves, and various other things I had to do for the job, all the while making small jabs at me. I didn't take anything she said personally, but it did piss me off to no end.

Once she finished showing me how to deal with new shipments, Robyn glanced at the clock.

"Do you work until three?" She asked.

"Yeah," I said. I hadn't realized how late it was already. "Are you on the same shift?"

She nodded.

"Come on, Tracy probably wants to talk to you before you leave," Robyn said. We walked back over to the office, and she knocked on the door. A moment later, Tracy called, "Come in!" and we went inside.

Tracy was sitting behind her desk with some paperwork in front of her.

"How did everything go today?" She asked.

"It was great," Robyn said with that stupid smile of hers. I generally wasn't a violent person, but I wanted to slap it off her face after the day we'd had.

Tracy turned her attention to me, so I nodded convincingly. "I learned a lot."

"Perfect!" Tracy said. "You can shadow Robyn tomorrow, and then you'll be ready to go."

That was not the news I wanted to hear, but I was clearly supposed to be happy about it.

"Great," I said.

"I look forward to it," Robyn said. She smiled in my direction, but her eyes were shooting daggers. I'm sure my face looked similar.

If there was one thing the two of us had always been good at, it was convincing adults that we got along well, even when we hated each other's guts.

❧

"How was work?" Kiara asked. I was lying on her bed while she hunted around her room for the various things she would need to take to camp (so much for her getting things done while I was at work).

"It was all right," I said. "You'll never guess who's working with me, though."

She slowed her movements and looked at me curiously.

"Who?" She asked.

"Robyn Huang."

"Robyn?" She asked. She sat on the edge of the bed. "That's awesome!"

I frowned. "No, it's not! I would be happy to go the rest of my life without seeing her again."

"You're just saying that because she beat you in the fifth-grade spelling bee."

I couldn't exactly deny that, but I didn't want her to think that was the only reason I was still mad at Robyn.

"Among other reasons," I muttered.

"We should go out for coffee or something," Kiara continued as if I hadn't said anything. "It would be so nice to catch up with her. I haven't seen her since middle school."

I sat up. "There is no way in hell I am hanging out with Robyn Huang."

Kiara rolled her eyes. "You're being petty."

"Petty? Petty, Kiara, is Robyn destroying my book because I was made eighth-grade valedictorian instead of her."

"She said it was an accident," Kiara defended.

"How do you accidentally drop a book in a lake, tear out half the pages, and ruin the remaining pages with dirt and spilled ink?"

Kiara hesitated. "Okay, maybe it was on purpose."

"You think?"

"But still, it was five years ago. Don't you think you should get over it by now?"

"I'll get over it when she apologizes and replaces the book."

"Come on, Harlee, she was thirteen years old. What can you expect her to do about it now?"

"I've already said what I want her to do," I said. "And before you say it, no, I don't think it is out of line for me to expect this, even if it has been five years."

"Fine. But I still want to hang out with her," Kiara said. She stood back up and continued throwing clothes into her duffel bag. "You two were friends at one point, remember."

"I was never friends with Robyn Huang," I muttered, spitting her name out. I knew what she was talking about. When we were really young, like five-years-old, Robyn and I would have play dates a lot. That was back when I was friends with everyone because that's just what kids do. But as soon as we started getting into competitive activities, we always ended up on different teams and our parents pretty much set us up against each other in everything. We competed in sports, as well as academic things like spelling bees. Our friendship fell apart pretty quickly after that since Robyn wasn't able to differentiate between our competition in activities and competition in our everyday lives. Suddenly, she was obsessed with beating me in every way she could. So although we were technically friends for that brief amount of time, I didn't really count it, and I didn't appreciate Kiara mentioning it.

"Well, I was friends with her," Kiara said, "and I want to see her again. Come or don't."

I glared at her. "We only have two weeks left together, and you want to spend it with Robyn Huang instead of me?"

She rolled her eyes. "You act like I'm going off to

war or something. Besides, I didn't say I want to spend time with her instead of you, just that I want to spend time with her too."

"Same thing."

"And why do you keep calling her by her full name?" Kiara asked. "It's like if I constantly called you Harlee Dunn."

"I'm sure that's what she calls me," I said. "It's always been a thing."

"I highly doubt she puts nearly this much energy into hating you," Kiara said.

Kiara was really oblivious to our rivalry if she felt that way. It was evident to me that Robyn had held on to her hate as much as I had. If she thought that was the case, though, then it was clear she wouldn't understand why I was still so angry about everything that happened between Robyn and me. She just didn't understand the situation, and why it was so important, so it was easier not to talk to her about it.

"Which bathing suits are you taking with you?" I asked. I shifted so I was lying on my stomach. "Only one-pieces, right?"

"Yeah, I was thinking these ones..."

We spent the next couple of hours chatting about random things, the topic of Robyn Huang never coming up again, although it was on my mind the entire time.

❧ 4 ❧

MY SECOND DAY of work was very similar to my first day. I was once again stuck with Robyn. The night before, after leaving Kiara's house, I'd promised myself that I would be civil with her at work for the sake of doing well at my job. The last thing I needed was to get fired for being unprofessional. Unfortunately, Robyn made it very difficult for me to do so.

"You were almost late this morning," she commented mildly as we began work.

"I was five minutes early."

She shrugged with one shoulder, her nose in the air like she thought she was so much better than me.

"I usually try to get here fifteen minutes early," she said. "It makes it easier for everyone, you know?"

Needless to say, I had to remind myself many times that I would lose my job if I screamed at her in the store.

Still, the training proved a little more useful than the day before. I was actually getting some hands-on work done, and while Robyn was definitely very rude when she corrected my mistakes, I at least felt like I could competently do the job.

"Now we're just going to make sure all the shelves are tidy," she said, leading me into the Teen and Young Adult section. "Sometimes people just pick up books and leave them around the store randomly, so we need to put them back."

I nodded along. I tried not to do anything like that for the sake of the employees who had to fix it, but I definitely did it occasionally.

A minute later, we passed by a large display.

"Remember when we were kids, and we read those books?" Robyn asked, waving her hand at the display. Her lip curled. "You were always so obsessed."

I narrowed my eyes. I didn't appreciate the tone or the suggestion that I was the only one who was obsessed with the series. It was the *Secret Tales* series, which had something like twenty-five books. Everyone in our grade used to love them. In our usual fashion, Robyn and I had turned our reading of the books into a competition to see who could finish them first. It didn't work out too well since we hadn't realized at the time that the series was still ongoing (and seemed to still be now, based on the display). Despite how much I liked the series, it was still very much a sore spot for me. My mom was friends with Robyn's mom, so she had forced me to lend Robyn a copy of the fifteenth book. My beautiful, brand-new, hardcover copy of the book that had just come out. Robyn had then destroyed it, and I was still angry about it to this day.

"Yeah," I said. "I remember."

Based on how she walked away without a care in the world, she didn't pick up on the anger in my tone. I continued walking after her, glaring daggers into her back. How the hell was I supposed to act civil when she was so awful?

"There's a new shipment of books we're going to have to deal with later," Robyn continued. "I think it's a new book in a fantasy series. Probably hardcover."

I probably shouldn't have said what I did next. I probably wouldn't have if it was anyone else.

"I'm surprised they let you deal with the hardback books," I said airily, "seeing as you're incapable of returning them to their rightful owner in proper condition."

Robyn's jaw clenched, and anger flashed in her eyes, but she didn't say anything. I was pleased to see that I didn't even need to say the name of the book or mention the incident for her to know what I was talking about. Clearly, she remembered our worst falling out too — which only proved that I was right and Kiara was wrong.

I clearly pissed Robyn off more than I had intended because she barely said two words to me for the rest of the day. Despite it being an unintended consequence of my words, I was very pleased with it. Maybe, after many years of trying, I had finally found a way to get Robyn Huang to just shut the fuck up.

AT THE END of the day, I went to the washroom to touch up my makeup before I met up with Kiara. It probably wasn't necessary, but I was honestly looking for any excuse to hang back so Robyn and I wouldn't have to walk out together. I waited a few minutes, until I was pretty much certain that she was gone, before I walked into the main part of the store again.

I was supposed to meet Kiara outside so we could bike over to the coffee shop down the road. We often ended up just spending time at our houses, but we decided since I was working over here anyway, we might as well try to go out a little more. To my surprise, I immediately spotted Kiara inside the store, near the front counter. She was talking to someone, but I couldn't see who it was from the angle I was standing at. I frowned. Was there something she needed in the store? Kiara wasn't a big reader, but it was possible she was looking for a gift or something.

When I got a little closer, Kiara looked over and

waved. I smiled in greeting. A moment later, I wished she hadn't noticed me standing there, though, because I saw who she was talking to. I slowed my steps as much as possible without looking like a total freak, but it didn't make any difference.

"Hey, Harlee!" Robyn said with a big smile. Or perhaps smirk was a better word for it.

"Great news, Harlee," Kiara said. "Robyn's going to join us."

Well, that's fantastic.

"I hope you don't mind," Robyn said.

I wouldn't mind stabbing pencils in your eyes. Okay — maybe that was a little too harsh.

"Of course not," I said. I was tempted to make up some excuse of why I couldn't go — I was fantastic at faking emergencies — but I knew Robyn would see straight through it, and I refused to give her the satisfaction of knowing that she got under my skin. "Are we still going to that coffee shop?"

"That's what I was thinking," Kiara said. She looked at Robyn. "Are you good with that?"

If she's not, she's welcome to leave.

"Of course," Robyn said. "Should we get going?"

Kiara glanced at me. Knowing that making some excuse of why I couldn't leave yet would only be delaying the inevitable, I nodded. Outside, all of our bikes were lined up next to each other.

"Do you not drive either?" Kiara asked Robyn as we headed out.

"No, I do," Robyn said. "But I don't have my own car, and my parents don't want me to take the family car to work every day."

We rode in a V formation, with Kiara and Robyn side-by-side and me hanging back. They happily chatted the whole way while I didn't say a single word. I wondered if either of them would notice if I just turned and went home instead.

For most of the way, Robyn was telling a story about her and her siblings from a few years ago.

"Anyway, then my brother just screamed that he hated me..." she said. Of course he did. Everyone hates you. "And my sister was being a brat, as usual..." *Takes one to know one.* "And my parents were..." *Honestly, does this girl ever shut up?*

Thankfully, the bike ride to the coffee shop was short. As soon as we got there, I ran inside to get my drink, leaving them in my dust, desperate to just have a little bit of space from Robyn. When they caught up to me, Kiara looked at me like I was crazy, but Robyn just laughed and said, "You need caffeine that badly?" I refused to dignify her with a response.

We sat down at a small table by the window. Kiara started asking Robyn questions about her first year of university, which naturally led Robyn to tell even more stories as if we cared about her life.

It took all of five minutes for me to get distracted. Robyn was telling a story about somebody on her residence floor who caused a fire alarm to go off, and I resisted the urge to roll my eyes. As if we all didn't have a story like that.

I quickly decided that people watching was much more interesting to Robyn, so I looked around the shop. There was a man sitting at the corner table, reading the newspaper. At another table, two girls were chatting while a black lab service dog laid beside one of them. I smiled when I caught sight of that, desperately wanting to go ask about the dog but knowing it would be incredibly rude to do so. There were no customers at the counter, so the baristas were chatting loudly while they cleaned up. I grinned wryly and wondered if they sometimes just pretending to be sweeping or wiping down the counters, so they could gossip at work. I knew I used to do that when I worked in retail.

I did my best to tune into their gossip while still ignoring Robyn and Kiara's conversation. From what I could tell, the workers were talking about their friend, Jessica's, boyfriend cheating on her and how she took him back anyway. Apparently, she'd been with the guy for years, and this had completely blind-sided her. The blonde worker said that Jessica could do better, while the brunette argued that she probably only took him back because they'd been together for so long that she didn't know how to live without him. And then, the real kicker, the redhead revealed that there was a rumour going around that he had actually gotten the other girl pregnant. I got so involved in this story that I gasped out loud when she said that.

Both Robyn and Kiara stared at me.

"What?" I asked. I was partially hoping one of them had said something gasp-worthy, but I assumed that wasn't the case based on their expressions.

"Why did you just gasp?" Kiara asked.

"Oh," I said. I gestured vaguely at the large window beside us. "I saw... a car almost hit a cyclist."

"Oh," Kiara said. She was still frowning at me, and

I got the sense that she didn't believe me. Which would be entirely fair, given I hadn't been looking out the window when I had gasped — it wasn't my best lie, by a long shot.

"Anyway," Robyn said.

Kiara turned her undivided attention back to her, and I went back to people watching. There was a small line of people waiting to order now, so the baristas weren't gossiping anymore, unfortunately. I looked at the other tables around us as much as I could without turning my head too much. I didn't mind looking slightly away from the table, but I knew Kiara would get annoyed if I turned my back on Robyn altogether to look around.

A teen in the corner was reading Pride & Prejudice, which reminded me of the book I had sitting in my bag. It was my second book of the week, and I really wanted to finish it that night. If I'd realized Kiara was going to invite Robyn along for this hangout, I would have said I was busy then gone home to read instead. It would have been a better use of my time, that was for sure. I was a little tempted to just pull the book out and read it, no matter how rude that would be. To a certain extent, I wanted to do it simply because it was rude — like *yeah, Robyn, I care so little about what you're saying or even seeming like I'm interested in it that I'm just going to read instead.* If this was some parallel universe where Robyn and I were hanging out alone, I would do it, but Kiara was here too, and I knew it would spark an argument between us. Kiara, similar to our other friend Bree, was polite to a fault.

She didn't appreciate me being mean or rude to anyone, even when it was well deserved.

I sighed and took a sip of my drink. I supposed I would just have to wait this one out.

I wouldn't say I was generally impatient, but my patience wore very thin, very fast sitting in that coffee shop. After five minutes, I was bouncing my leg incredibly fast, just for something to do. After ten minutes, my head was beginning to ache. After twenty minutes, now with a full-blown headache, I was debating whether that was a good enough excuse to leave. I decided it wasn't, at least not yet, since Robyn would inevitably think I was going because of her, and I could not let that happen.

Thankfully, the choice to leave didn't need to be mine. I zoned back in to the conversation when Robyn said, "Well, this has been tons of fun, but I need to get home."

"Of course," Kiara said. "We should meet up again soon!"

I wondered if anyone but me would be able to hear the insecurity in her voice as she said that.

"Definitely," Robyn said. "What's your phone number?"

Kiara recited her number, and Robyn put it in her phone, then texted her to make sure it was right. Once Kiara confirmed that it was, Robyn waved and walked off. Fucking finally.

"Why were you being so rude?" Kiara snapped as soon as Robyn left the shop.

I raised my eyebrows. "Excuse me?"

"Robyn was being perfectly nice, and you just

ignored her for the whole time she was here. You probably hurt her feelings."

"Well, maybe if you wanted me to engage with her, you should have warned me she was coming," I said. I crossed my arms. "You're the one who sprung this on me."

"I didn't mean to spring it on you. It just naturally came up when I saw her at the store," Kiara said. "What was I supposed to do? Say I was hanging out with you then not invite her?"

"You didn't need to mention it!"

"She asked me why I was at the store."

"Then lie!" I snapped. Kiara flinched back in surprise at my tone. I took a couple of deep breaths to get myself under control again. Slowly, I said, "What I mean is that I made it clear to you that I don't want to be friends with Robyn. You can do whatever you want, but you can't force me to go along with it."

"I guess that's fair," Kiara conceded. "But for the record, I think you're being childish by holding on to this grudge."

"Noted," I said through gritted teeth.

"And," Kiara said loudly, "I think it would be better for everyone, including you, if you just let it go."

I glared at her. "That's not for you to decide."

❧

"I'm home," I called as I dragged myself into my house later that evening. Things had been tense between Kiara and me after Robyn left, and between that and my headache, I was just about ready to explode by the time we decided to go home. I dropped my bag, kicked off my shoes by the front door, and then walked into the kitchen.

"Hi, sweetie," my mom said. She was wrangling Emery into a T-shirt. "We're just leaving for Greyson's soccer game. We'll be back in a couple of hours."

"Okay," I said. I didn't understand how Greyson feasibly had this many soccer games — it was like they were daily.

"I left money for dinner on the counter," Mom said. She patted my shoulder as she walked by, pulling Emery along with her. In usual six-year-old fashion, he was screaming about how he didn't want to go, but she didn't pay that any mind.

"Where's Dad?" I had to raise my voice to ask it over Emery's yelling. That boy had a real set of lungs on him.

"He's already in the car," Mom said. I guess I had walked right past him without noticing. She grabbed her house key and then walked outside. "Love you!"

"Love you!" I called back absentmindedly as I thought about what I wanted to do for the evening.

I fell onto the couch and groaned. It felt so good to be lying down after being on my feet all day. That was definitely a large adjustment of the job for me. I turned on the TV. Some random sitcom was playing, and I just dropped the remote, leaving it to play. I didn't particularly care what I watched right now, it was just some nice background noise.

During the commercial break, I thought over what Kiara had said in the coffee shop. Was I being childish for holding on to my grudge against Robyn? I thought I'd adequately explained my reasoning to her, so I didn't understand why she seemed to feel so strongly about it. Really, why should I have to forgive Robyn when she had never apologized and was being as insufferable as usual?

My general philosophy in life was that indifference is the best revenge — it had served me well over the years and helped me make sure that I wasn't giving energy to someone who didn't deserve it. In theory, I supposed Robyn could fit in that category, but there was something about her that made me unable to do that. Sure, over the past five years, I hadn't actively thought about her and hated her, but now that I had to see her every day, I didn't see there being any way that I could just ignore my feelings. I certainly didn't see why I should have to just because it was easier for Kiara.

I sighed and turned the TV off again. I hated dwelling on stuff like this, especially in my time off. I would just talk to Kiara about it later and explain to her in no uncertain terms that it was up to me how I felt about and treated Robyn. In the meantime, I pulled out a book and began reading again. I couldn't let myself fall behind on this goal.

$\maltese$ 6 $\maltese$

My FIRST DAY working on my own did not go as well as planned. I was a little unsure of how prepared I was, given Robyn hadn't really taught me anything during my training, but I am nothing if not a master of convincing people I know what I'm doing when I'm really lost. For the morning, this worked well. I felt confident in my abilities, and when Tracy asked me how my day was going, I could honestly say it was great.

Then the afternoon happened.

"Excuse me?" A woman said, tapping me on the shoulder. I turned around to look at her. She was a little on the older side and looked unsure of what she was doing.

"Can I help you?" I asked politely.

"Yes, I'm looking for a book." I smiled and nodded, waiting for her to elaborate, but she just looked at me expectantly.

"Okay, that's great," I said. "Are you looking for a

particular book, or do you want a recommendation? Or are you looking for a specific part of the store?"

I did my best to ask open-ended questions, not wanting to assume what she was looking for, but she just huffed and crossed her arms.

"I'm looking for a specific book," she said, then stared at me as if she wanted me to make the book appear from thin air. I had to bite back the words I wanted to say, which were akin to asking how the fuck she wanted me to find the one book she wanted in an entire bookstore when she had given me no way of knowing which book she wanted.

"Okay," I said, trying to remain calm and helpful. "Do you know the title of the book?"

"No," she said shortly.

"All right. Do you know the author or the genre? I can help you find the area the book would be sold in."

"No, I don't know any of that," she said, waving her hand around. She squinted at me. "You do work here, don't you? Isn't it your job to help people find books?"

Not like this.

"I'm happy to help you find the book, ma'am, but I need some more details about what you're looking for if you want me to help you find it."

"It's just a book!" She snapped. "What is so hard about that?"

"I can help you find that, ma'am," Robyn said. Where the hell had she come from?

"That's all right," I said with a tight smile. "I have no problem helping her."

"You're taking too long," Robyn muttered. She

smiled brightly at the woman. "What do you need help looking for?"

"A book!" The woman said impatiently as if we weren't in a book full of them.

"Of course, ma'am," Robyn said. "Do you have a specific genre you're looking for, or a title or author, perhaps?"

"I don't know," she said. "It's a romance of some sort. Has an attractive man on the cover."

That narrowed it down to pretty much anything in the adult romance section.

"Why don't we step over to the romance section, and we can see if we can find what you're looking for?" Robyn suggested.

Once she was far enough away, I rolled my eyes. Did she think I was unable to do my job, or was she just trying to be annoying? Probably both, knowing her. Still, I didn't care that much since she had technically saved me from that woman. I wasn't about to thank her for it or anything, but I was willing to push the interaction to the back of my mind so I could focus on work. I tried to, at least, until it happened again.

"You can find all of his works in the Young Adult section," I told the customer, who had come in asking about some famous author. "It's at the end of the store there."

"Do you have his most recent book in stock?" The customer asked. I opened my mouth to say that yes, we probably did since there was a large display of it when Robyn appeared by my side.

"I can check on that on the computer, if you'd

like," she said smoothly. She gently guided the customer over to the computer so they could look it up. I stared at them for a moment before I spun on my heel and walked away.

"Quit stopping me from doing my job," I said when Robyn walked near me later.

"Get better at your job, and I will," she said, without stopping to look at me.

How am I supposed to get better at my job when you're there?

In her typical fashion, Robyn did not stop. It was probably my fault a little since I couldn't stop myself from showing my annoyance at the situation, which was exactly what Robyn wanted. I was about ready to scream by the end of my shift. It wasn't that I really cared about dealing with customers — I *was* working for minimum wage in retail — I was just pissed that Robyn was making it seem like I couldn't do my job. My only hope was that Tracy hadn't noticed.

"Better luck tomorrow, Harlee," Robyn said as we walked out.

I didn't have a good comeback, so I just said, "Fuck off," got on my bike and rode away.

❦   7   ❦

MY DAY MIGHT HAVE BEEN stressful, but that didn't mean I was going to skip a FaceTime call with my best friends. There were five of us in all: me, Kiara, April, Elyssa, and Bree. Earlier in the month, we'd gone on a road trip together (which was quite an adventure, let me tell you), and soon after we got back, Elyssa suggested we set up a weekly video call. Save for Kiara and me, we all lived very far apart, and there was a good chance we wouldn't see each other again until we got back to school in the fall, so this would be the perfect way for us to keep up with one another.

So on Wednesday night, after telling my parents and brothers in no uncertain terms that I did not want to be disturbed while I was on my call, I holed up in my bedroom with my laptop. I may have only been three days into working, but I desperately needed to talk to somebody other than my coworkers.

"Hey, guys!" Elyssa said once we were all connected. "How's it going?"

Nobody looked too eager to share, which was a little concerning to me. While April and I weren't really people to spill our feelings, especially over a call like this, Bree and Kiara were big talkers. Things were still pretty tense between Kiara and me since I hadn't had the chance to talk to her again since the day before when we'd had our minor argument, so that might have been why she wasn't jumping at the chance to talk right now. The thought of that made me feel a little guilty.

Bree, bless her, broke the silence. "I'm pretty good."

Elyssa smiled widely. "Good." Nobody said anything for a moment. "How about you, April?"

April pointed at herself questioningly, as if there was anyone else in the call Elyssa could have been talking to. Elyssa nodded encouragingly like a teacher trying to coax a shy student into speaking in front of the class.

"I'm good as well," April said.

"Missing Bree?" Kiara asked.

"Always," April replied immediately. That was a little dramatic, but I understood the sentiment. The two of them had only been dating for two weeks, so they were probably still in the perfect honeymoon stage, but they were in different cities and could only visit each other on weekends. Bree blew a kiss at the screen, which I assumed was directed at April. I grimaced. Although I'd been rooting for them to end up together while we were on our road trip earlier that summer, having to watch them be sickeningly sweet in front of us was not my idea of a good time.

"How about Kiara and Harlee?" Elyssa asked. I straightened at my name. "How are you?"

I looked at Kiara on the screen, though I suppose she wouldn't be able to tell that, willing her to answer the question first. I didn't know how much she wanted to share with our friend group, so I found it easier to just follow her lead on this.

"I'm pretty good," Kiara said. "Just hanging out for the next week and a half."

"Ah yes, the chronicles of Kiara waiting to go to camp continue," Bree said dramatically.

"I wonder what will happen on today's episode," April added in a similar tone.

Kiara smiled. "Sorry if I talk about it too much. I'm just excited."

"It's never too much," Bree said, shaking her head.

"Let's just say, we've never had to wonder what job you're working this summer," April said. I laughed. Within a moment, I regretted that, as everyone's attention turned towards me.

"You're being awfully quiet, Harlee," Elyssa said. She was playing with an elastic band, and I found it really distracting. "Lost in thought?"

"When is she not?" April asked.

"I prefer listening," I said.

"Well, you have to talk sometimes on these calls!" Bree said, waggling her finger. "How's your life going?"

"Not much has changed in the two weeks since I last saw you," I said honestly. "I started work a couple days ago. That's been fun."

Kiara made a face at my words, but she didn't say anything. Luckily, nobody else seemed to notice.

"I thought you started work next week," April said. Her eyebrows scrunched together in thought. "Am I getting those dates right? I can't do math."

"Of course you can't, you're gay," Bree quipped immediately. I snorted.

"I was supposed to start next Monday," I said. "But my boss asked me to start early, and I had no reason to say no."

"Make that coin," Bree said with a grin.

"You like the job?" Elyssa asked.

Remembering Robyn and the day we had, I couldn't honestly say yes. I shrugged. "It's a job."

"Oh, by the way," Bree said. She reached out of frame then held up a large cardboard box so we could all see it. "Did one of you send this package to my house?"

We did, actually, though it was supposed to arrive a while ago. It was a present we'd gotten her for her birthday.

"Yeah!" Kiara said.

"It's a box of bees," April said with a straight face. "Happy two-week anniversary."

"Thank you so much, babe," Bree said. She dropped the box again. "I'll open that later so you don't all have to watch me get killed by a thousand bees."

"Don't worry, they're not trained to attack you," Kiara said.

"Somehow, I don't think you can control that," Bree said.

"The guy we bought them from said they were the kindest bees he owns," I added on.

"His site is down now, and I saw on the news that he went to prison, but he seemed really nice," Kiara said.

"We should send him a care package in prison for providing us with such a wonderful service," Bree said dryly.

"But where would we get the bees for the care package?" Elyssa asked.

April snorted. "We'll have to find a new supplier. Anyone know someone?"

"Wait, I actually got an ad for that this morning," Elyssa said. She shared her screen and opened a screenshot. I laughed a little in surprise: right there, it said GET LIVE BEES. 2 DAY DELIVERY.

"It knows," April said ominously.

"It could see your search history," Bree said. The screen changed so we could see Elyssa again.

"What makes you think I was the one who bought them?" Elyssa asked. She sounded a little hurt, though I imagined it was just for show. Out of everyone in our friend group, Elyssa was definitely the sweetest and purest, so the idea of her buying live bees was pretty laughable.

"It's always the quiet ones."

"Finally, someone agrees with me!" April said. "I was always a little worried Elyssa was going to kill me in my sleep."

"What?" Elyssa screeched. April and Elyssa were roommates in residence during our first year of university. While they got along very well, there was no denying they were an unusual pair.

"I'm kidding, E," April said soothingly. "Well—kind of."

Elyssa did not look soothed. "Harlee is more likely to kill you than I am."

"Rude," I said, though I couldn't really argue it. If my feelings about Robyn showed me anything, it was that I could hold a grudge, and I was definitely pretty vindictive. I would never kill someone, of course, but in a group of people who would never kill someone, I was probably the most likely to do it.

"No, no, she's right," Kiara said. I flipped her off, but all that did was make everyone laugh. "But for legal reasons, this is all a joke." She stared into the distance seriously, like she was looking at an imaginary camera.

"Stop pretending you're on The Office," April said. She threw a couple pieces of popcorn at the camera as if they would hit Kiara through the screen. Kiara flinched back, though I honestly couldn't tell if it was on purpose or not. After that, everything quickly derailed into a "food fight," or as much of a food that you can have over FaceTime.

It was very chaotic, but it was also the perfect way for me to forget my awful day.

⚜   8   ⚜

IF THERE WAS one thing Kiara and I were good at, it was pretending our arguments never happened. Granted, we rarely had severe arguments. The few times we did, they officially ended within a couple days, when one of us bought the other a small reconciliation gift, like a coffee or a book.

Our argument about Robyn was luckily minor enough that there was no gift necessary. Any excess tension was dissipated in our call with April, Bree, and Elyssa, and by Thursday morning, everything was back to normal.

And this time, she warned me in advance that she was inviting Robyn over after work.

The day had been another long and exhausting one. It had been four days since I'd started working with Robyn, and I was definitely ready for the weekend when I wouldn't have to see her for a whole forty-eight hours.

Kiara and Robyn rode their bikes side-by-side and

talked the whole way. I was behind them yet again and tried to imagine that I was doing something, anything, else. Realistically, I could have just gone home and spent my evening doing something more enjoyable than hating Robyn Huang with all my might, but I didn't want to bail on Kiara, even if I was a little angry with her. Granted, she probably wouldn't notice my absence since she was having such a good time with Robyn, but I would still feel bad ditching her right before she left for two months straight.

"We should go swimming while we're at my place," Kiara said.

"I don't have my bathing suit," Robyn replied.

"That's too bad," I said flatly, "maybe next time."

"That's okay!" Kiara said, completely ignoring me. "I have tons of extras. I'm sure we can find one that fits you."

"Really? That's so sweet of you, thanks!"

Yeah, so sweet of you, Kiara. Couldn't have just cut me a break on this one time.

I did feel a little bit guilty for some of the thoughts that I had. Kiara was just being her typical sweet self, which was something I loved her for, and I was there just trampling all over it. But I couldn't help it. Robyn pissed me off in a way that nobody else could.

I didn't have a bathing suit either, so all three of us went upstairs to find some from Kiara's room. Robyn and I could have easily just gone home to get our own bathing suits, but despite having a small population, our town was very spread out, so it would have taken a good amount of time. I immediately took the black one-piece with cut-outs that I wore every time I borrowed Kiara's stuff and went into the bathroom to get changed. I would have been fine getting changed in front of Kiara, but I didn't really feel like changing in front of Robyn. When I got back, both of them were dressed as well, so we grabbed towels and went downstairs.

It was a pretty warm day, so I didn't even entertain the possibility of going in the hot tub. As soon as we got outside, I dove straight into the pool. Robyn and Kiara did the same a moment after me.

"Hey, Kiara, do you have any of the floats inflated?" I asked. Her family had a collection of them, but we always forgot to inflate them before we got in the water.

Her face lit up. "Yeah, I think so! Let me go grab them."

She climbed out and ran over to the garage, leaving Robyn and me alone. I would have been happy to sit in silence, but Robyn clearly had other ideas.

"I'm surprised you and Kiara are still friends after all these years," she said mildly.

"Why?" I asked disinterestedly. "We've always been best friends."

She shrugged. "You're just really different. Kiara is so sweet and nice, and you're... well, you're you."

I pushed myself off the wall I'd been leaning against.

"And what's that supposed to mean?" I asked dangerously.

"I found some!" Kiara called, coming out of the garage. Robyn and I immediately broke eye contact, and I tried to look happy for Kiara's sake. Robyn climbed out of the pool to help Kiara pull the large floats over. She had the yellow duck, the flamingo, and the watermelon. All three of them were the kind that had a hole in the middle, so you could either sit in it or have it wrapped around you.

"Can I have the flamingo?" Robyn asked. They slid all the floats into the pool, but she held onto the rubber neck of the flamingo.

"Sure," Kiara said. She tried to push the duck to me, though it didn't make it very far, and I had to swim over. We all opted to sit on the floats, using our hands to move us around as needed.

"Hey, you know what I was thinking about the other day?" Robyn said. To my surprise, she was looking at me. "I remembered that like back when we were in like seventh grade, we would compete to see who could finish more book reports every year."

Kiara frowned in thought. "Was that the thing where we had to do at least one every month but would get small prizes if we did more?"

"Yeah," I said.

"I did the most in the class by the end of the year," Robyn said.

"But I did more the next year," I responded. We both said it so casually — as if it meant nothing when we both knew it meant everything.

"Gosh, that feels like forever ago," Kiara said, oblivious to what we were doing. "I wonder how everyone from our class is now. I haven't seen so many of them in years."

That, of course, turned the conversation to a less

competitive one. I hadn't kept up with anyone but Kiara in the year since we'd graduated high school, so I had nothing to contribute to the conversation, but Robyn seemed to know everyone, based on how long she talked for.

I was getting a little too warm, sitting only half in the water like I was, so I jumped out of my float and stayed underwater for as long as I could. When I was younger, I'd done synchronized swimming, so I used to be able to hold my breath for incredible lengths of time, but that wasn't the case anymore. I think I managed to stay under for about twenty seconds before my chest felt like it was on fire, and I had to come up for air.

"Not your best time," Kiara said.

"I know," I replied. This was a game we played. Whenever I went underwater, she would keep track of how long I managed to stay under. We'd started the game when we were in elementary school, and to this day, my best record was from when I was ten and managed to stay underwater for a little over a minute.

"I'm cold," Robyn said. "I'm going to tan for a bit."

"I'll join you," Kiara said. They both slipped back into the water and swam over to the side. Out of habit, I followed.

There were three lounge chairs by the side of the pool, like they were made for us. Kiara laid back on the chair in the middle while I went on her right and Robyn went on her left. It was already a warm day, and with the sun beating down on us, I felt like I was in a sauna. I almost fell asleep lying there.

"So, you leave for camp next week, Kiara?" Robyn

asked, breaking the silence. My hand clenched into a fist involuntarily. She couldn't even let me relax.

"A week from Sunday," Kiara said in a chipper voice.

"That's exciting. Have you worked there before?"

"This is my fourth summer working there," Kiara said. She said it guiltily like she thought she shouldn't be working at a camp for that many years.

"Wow, four years," Robyn said. "You must really like it there."

"I do."

"Are you working as a counsellor?"

"Yep! Well, technically, I'm the head counsellor of the age group I'm working with. This is my first year with that title. I'm a little nervous."

"I'm sure you'll do great," Robyn said confidently. "Do you have any plans for the summer, Harlee?"

"No," I said flatly. What kind of plans would I have? I was just working with her all summer.

"What she means to say," Kiara said in a pointed tone, "is that she doesn't have any vacations or anything planned for the summer. She's working the whole time."

"Well, that can be fun too," Robyn said. "I'm doing the same."

Fucking great.

"You know, Harlee's doing a pretty intense reading challenge this summer," Kiara said.

"Oh?" Robyn asked. She was clearly feigning her interest. I wasn't sure why she bothered; I knew she didn't care.

"Yeah," Kiara said. My eyes were closed, but I

could hear her shifting around like she turned to lie on her side and face Robyn. "She has this crazy long list of books she wants to read, so she's trying to read a bunch of them before the end of summer. How many was it again, Harlee?"

"About fifty," I muttered.

"Fifty," Robyn said. I think she was trying to sound impressed, but she failed miserably. "That's a lot."

"Like you can do better," I snapped. I opened my eyes to look at her. She was also lying on her side.

She tapped her chin in thought. "Fifty... Yeah, I bet I could do more than that."

"Really?" Kiara asked. "I'm pretty sure I can't even read fifty books in an entire year, let alone a summer."

I ignored her in favour of staring at Robyn. I had a choice to make here: Robyn was clearly challenging me, and she was waiting to see if I took her up on it. If I brushed it off, then she would think that she won. If I agreed to it, there was a chance that she would show me up in the future, but there was also a chance that I would win — and I was always looking for a way to beat Robyn Huang.

"Why don't we put it to the test?" I suggested.

Kiara groaned. "Oh no."

Robyn tilted her head in interest, a smile playing on her lips. I'd clearly walked right into her trap, but there was no backing out now.

"We both keep track of how many books we read by the end of the summer," I said. "Whoever loses owes the winner ten bucks."

Sure, ten dollars wasn't much. It was less than either of us made in an hour. But it wasn't about the prize money — it was about our dignity. The money just made it feel a little more official.

"What are we calling the end of summer?" Robyn asked.

I thought about it for a moment. I'd realized the day before that I counted my weeks wrong and actually had eleven weeks left from the time I'd started counting, not nine, but I didn't want to bother changing that goal.

"August fifteenth," I said. "It's an even eight weeks from now."

"You're on," Robyn said. She reached her hand out. She was still wet from the pool, so some water dropped off her wrist onto Kiara beneath her. Paying that no mind, I shook her hand. Kiara rolled her eyes but didn't say anything.

After that, we went back to tanning in silence, though Robyn now had a smug smirk on her face.

❧

Like the other day in the coffee shop, as soon as Robyn left, Kiara rounded on me.

"Why the hell would you make that bet?" She asked.

"What are you talking about?" I asked. I switched to lying on my stomach, so my back could get some sun.

"The bet you just made with Robyn," she said. I rolled my eyes; it wasn't that I hadn't known which bet she was talking about. I just didn't see why she cared.

"She was the one who brought it up."

"You suggested the bet."

"She was pretty much begging for me to when she said she could read more than me."

"You didn't need to push it!"

"Why do you care so much, Kiara?" I asked loudly. "It's literally just a reading competition, and the worst that happens is I owe her ten bucks."

True, I did think it meant more than that to both Robyn and me, but that wouldn't have helped my argument with Kiara, so I chose not to bring that up.

"I'm worried about you obsessing over Robyn."

"I'm not obsessing over her!"

"All you've done since you started work is talk about how much you hate her."

"Well, maybe I wouldn't need to do that if you stopped inviting her everywhere."

She threw her hands up. "Sorry, I want to spend time with my friend!"

"Why do you think I'm hanging out with the two of you?" I sat up. "I want to spend time with you. I don't want to spend time with Robyn. I've compromised by hanging out with both of you because you want to spend time with her. Part of what comes with that is me getting annoyed with her." My tone seeping with sarcasm, I added, "Sorry if that bothers you."

She stared at me. While Kiara and I frequently had minor spats, we rarely had significant arguments or ones that lasted more than one day. This was an anomaly, and I wasn't sure if either of us knew how to deal with it.

"I'm just worried that this competition is going to bring out the worst in you," Kiara said softly.

"Literally, all we're going to be doing is reading," I said. I was getting frustrated with her, despite her good intentions. It was like she thought me doing anything near Robyn would end with me killing someone — while simultaneously inviting her everywhere. "And that's beside the point, anyway. Why do you want me to change when you think Robyn is just perfect as she is?"

"I don't think she's perfect—"

"Just that she's better than me," I said flatly. We stared at each other in silence. Usually, I would break it by changing the subject, but honestly, I wanted her to see what she was doing.

"I didn't mean for you to think that."

"Kiara..." I paused, trying to collect my thoughts. "I can promise you that Robyn hates me just as much as I hate her. She just doesn't talk to you about it because you're not her best friend."

"Can't you please just make an effort?" She asked. "I like you both. I want to spend time with you both."

"I can be civil," I said. "But I won't be her friend."

"Okay," Kiara said quickly. "Okay, I'll take that."

I nodded and laid back down. She did the same. The air was still tense, though, and I needed to break it somehow.

"What do you think your dad's going to make us for dinner?" I asked. I was staying over at her house for dinner, as I often did, since my parents weren't going to be home for the fourth night in a row.

Kiara smiled. "I don't know. He mentioned a few different ideas to me this morning..."

She continued talking, and I smiled and laughed along. Because nothing was ever that serious between Kiara and me.

❧

I was already waking up pretty early every morning to go to work, but the following day, I woke up even earlier than usual, so I had time to read before work. I was already halfway through a book, and my hope was to finish it before I left the house. I was a little over-optimistic with that plan, though. Despite reading as I did everything in the morning (making breakfast with one hand was more difficult than I'd anticipated), I only made it about three-quarters of the way through the book by the time I had to leave for work. I briefly considered reading as I biked since I was pretty at reading while I walked, but I quickly surmised that would be way too dangerous.

Still, I didn't give up on the goal. During every break that I had, I turned back to reading the book. I even read when the store was pretty empty — sure, I wasn't technically doing my job, but hey, what can you expect from minimum wage employees?

I finally finished the book right at the beginning of my lunch break and turned to rub it in Robyn's face that I was already done reading one book, but she wasn't there. I guess she was still on the floor. Unperturbed, I just pulled out my phone and logged the book as read on Goodreads. My summer goal was a little messed up by this competition since I was starting from zero books as of last night, so that it was fair, but I didn't mind that so much when I could see clearly that I was ahead of Robyn.

Harlee - 1. Robyn - 0.

9

THAT AFTERNOON, Kiara came to the store yet again. I knew she was going to come by, but we didn't have any plans outside of that. I told her we could do what she wanted as long as she came prepared with some ideas.

As usual, Robyn and I finished work and walked outside at the same time. I wouldn't say we left together since we both tried to put as much distance between us as possible and didn't say a word the entire way across the parking lot to the bike rack. Kiara was sitting on a bench beside the rack but stood up when she saw us walk over.

"Hey, guys!" She said enthusiastically. "How was work?"

"It was okay," I said, immediately getting to unlocking my bike.

"Pretty good," Robyn said. "Not too busy."

"A lot of people leave town on Fridays," Kiara says.

Robyn closed her eyes and turned her face to the sky, letting the warm sun hit it.

"I would just love to go on vacation right now," she said. "Somewhere warm and tropical."

"It's finally summer in Canada, and you want to leave?" Kiara asked with a small laugh.

Robyn looked at her again. "Good point. I guess I should save that plan for the dead of winter."

Kiara laughed. "Oh, by the way, Harlee and I are going to see a movie tomorrow night. We," Kiara looked at me pointedly, daring me to argue, "would love it if you joined."

I was starting to feel like a kid whose parent was trying to make friends for them.

"Oh, that's so nice of you," Robyn said, "but I've actually got plans."

"Oh well, next time," I said. I grabbed Kiara's wrist and tried to pull her over to her bike, but she kept her feet planted firmly in the ground.

"What kind of plans?" Kiara asked. For a moment, I thought she was suspicious of Robyn's excuse, and I was interested to see if she was trying to catch Robyn in a lie, but that wasn't really Kiara's style. She was just genuinely interested in Robyn's life, which was a lot more boring for me.

"I have a date," Robyn said. She swayed a little from side to side, and if it was anyone else, I would say she was blushing.

"That's awesome!" Kiara said, clapping her hands together. "Who is it?"

Robyn waved her hand in the air in a dismissive manner.

"Nobody you know," she said. "Her name is Celine."

"So exciting!" Kiara said. "Where are you taking her? What are you going to wear?"

Robyn giggled. She actually giggled. I had never seen her act like this before, and honestly, I found it a little confusing. Robyn never struck me as particularly girly — that was one of the ways that she and I differed.

"We're just going to dinner," she said. "I'm not sure where. She's picking the place. And I was thinking of wearing..."

Despite my love of all things fashion, I zoned out. I did not want to hear about Robyn's dating life whatsoever. Who would want to date her anyway? Unfortunately for me, Robyn droned on about this girl and the date they were going on for fifteen minutes, and it looked like Kiara was entranced by her words. Finally, when I thought I might actually die in that parking lot because we were standing there for so long, Robyn said she had to go home.

"Are you working the weekend?" She asked.

"No," I said. "Tracy said all my shifts would be Monday to Friday."

"Oh," Robyn said. "Me too. Guess we'll be working together a lot this summer."

Fantastic. The one upside to it was that she looked just as displeased about the prospect as I did.

"See you Monday," I said. Kiara was a master of drawing out a goodbye, but I was more than ready for this week to be over.

"See ya," Robyn said. She rode away.

"Alright, to the mall," Kiara said.

"Remind me why we're going to the mall today when we're going again tomorrow for the movie?" I asked as we left the parking lot.

"Because I want to try the new bubble tea place, and I don't want to do that on the same day that I get popcorn."

"Because..." I prompted since I didn't see any issue with that.

"Because the flavours don't mix, you savage," she said. She looked at me with a grimace on her face. "Tapioca pearls and buttery popcorn? No thanks."

"You don't have to eat them at the same time!"

"The flavour will stay in my mouth!"

I still didn't see the big deal, but I relented since I had nothing better to do that evening anyway. This was good. This was how everything was supposed to be. Just me and Kiara without Robyn here to ruin everything.

Okay, maybe it felt a little weird to bike side-by-side again and for there to only be two of us instead of three, but I ignored that feeling because I finally had my best friend to myself again. It was just as well that Robyn was going on a date the next day — if everything went well between her and Celine, then maybe Robyn would have less time to spend with us.

❈

We spent a little over an hour at the mall before we went back to Kiara's house. She insisted that she needed to keep packing, and I was starting to wonder just how much she was planning to take to camp with her. I only went to camp for a few years, but I distinctly remembered packing the day before most of the time.

"Have you packed at all?" I asked when we were back in her room. I pointed accusingly at the bathing suits in her hand. "You already packed your bathing suits! I was here; I saw you do it!"

"I did pack them," she said.

"Aha, I knew it!"

Ignoring me, she continued, "I had to unpack them because I realized I needed them this week. Now I'm repacking them again."

"You do realize that you still have another week left before you go?"

"So?"

"So, if you needed those bathing suits this week, why do you think you won't need them next week too?"

Kiara sighed loudly and dropped the suits. "Damn it, Harlee!" She spun on her heel and went back to the closet.

I laughed at her theatrics.

"Sorry," I said, "but at least I saved you the pain of unpacking again."

She just sighed loudly again. I was now beginning to understand why it was taking her so long to pack. She got into the zone of doing stuff again and wasn't really talking to me, so I grabbed the extra book I'd packed in my bag and started reading it.

After I finished about two chapters, Kiara came and tilted the book upward so she could see the cover.

"That's not the same book you were reading last night," she said.

"I know," I said. I pulled it out of her grasp so I could continue reading. "I finished that one at lunch."

Kiara whistled. "Wow, you're reading fast."

I glared at her. "I have to read fast now that I'm in a reading competition with Robyn."

"Why are you acting like that's my fault?" She asked. She turned away and kept working. "You're the one who suggested the bet with her."

"We went over this. I wouldn't have even had the idea for the bet if you hadn't brought up the reading challenge when we were with Robyn."

I glanced at the time then went back to reading. If I didn't have to make dinner tonight and I was willing to stay up just a little later than usual, I could probably finish the book that night.

About ten minutes later, Kiara flopped down on the bed beside me.

"I give up!" She cried. "I will never finish packing."

"What's your plan, then? Leaving it until the last minute as usual?"

"I guess so," Kiara said with her trademark dramatic sigh. Clearly, my peace and quiet for reading was over, so I dog-eared my page, then rolled on my back like her.

"You'll get everything done," I said. "You always do."

We laid in silence for a minute.

"I'm really going to miss you, Harlee."

"You're only leaving for eight weeks, Kiara. Somehow, I think we'll manage."

"I don't know," she said. "I think I may die without you."

"What a shame," I said drily.

"You're so mean to me."

"We have this conversation every year." She didn't respond immediately, and I wondered if she was actually a little upset, so I added, "And we'll write letters to each other, just like you want."

She would have her phone with her for the whole summer, but she liked the "camp feel" of writing and receiving letters.

"It won't be the same."

"You say that every year, too," I said. I turned my head, so I was looking at her. "But I'll miss you too."

❧ 10 ❧

I HAD nothing to do for the entire day on Saturday before going to the movies with Kiara. It was my first day off since starting work, and my automatic instinct was to spend the whole day watching TV, but I quickly shot that idea down. I was still two books behind for the week, so reading was my top priority.

Before I got sucked into any book, I checked Goodreads so I could keep track of my competition with Robyn. We had both read two books since making the bet, leaving us neck and neck. If I was lucky, Robyn wouldn't read much over the weekend, and I would be able to pull ahead with just the two books. I didn't like relying on luck, though. It was probably better if I tried to read three books, just in case.

I was a relatively fast reader, but even that speed was pushing it for me a little. I looked over my bookshelf for anything that I'd been meaning to read for a while that was under 300 pages. Finally, I caught sight of a novella I wanted to read — Robyn and I hadn't specified anything about the competition, which meant that anything was fair game in my mind, including novellas.

I quickly wrote a sign that said *DO NOT DISTURB. I MEAN IT.* and stuck it to my door in the hopes that my family wouldn't bother me. It was probably a long shot that nobody would knock, but maybe the sign would make them think twice before trying to talk to me. If all went well, that would weed out any unimportant conversations.

Finally, feeling comfortable that I could probably read the novella and most of the novel that day, I settled into my chair and started reading.

11

KIARA and I didn't want to bike all the way to the mall for the second day in a row, so she went to ask her mom if she could drive us. She said yes but that she needed to go get groceries right afterward, so she would have to drop us off a little early. We would have to leave the house at the same time, either way, so we readily agreed. That is how we ended up outside the movie theatre more than forty-five minutes early.

"Sorry," the bored teenager working at the ticket booth said. "You can buy the tickets now, but there's still another movie playing in the theatre."

Let me tell you, I've been early to the movies but never so early that we couldn't even go inside yet. We bought our tickets anyway then decided to walk around for a bit to kill time. Typically, we would go into the used books and DVD store, but I wasn't exactly in the mood after spending all week working in a bookstore.

"We could get ice cream," Kiara suggested.

"You won't have bubble tea on the same day as popcorn, but ice cream is fine?"

She shook a deep breath like she was getting ready to argue, then deflated.

"Yeah, good point."

"Well, maybe we could—"

"Hey, look, there's Robyn!" Kiara said, completely cutting me off. She pointed down the hall. "Let's go say hi!"

She started to walk over, but I yanked her back.

"Are you crazy?" I hissed. "We can't go talk to her!"

Kiara tilted her head. "Why not?"

"She's on a date, Kiara! How would you feel if your friends came and interrupted your first date with someone?"

"Oh," she said. Her face fell. "Right. I forgot she was on a date."

I felt a little bad that she had been so excited to talk to Robyn but couldn't go and see her.

"Don't worry," I said. "I'm sure she'll tell you all about it next time you meet up."

Kiara nodded. "Yeah. I can't wait." Then her face brightened so much that it made me a little worried. "But why wait to hear about how her date went?"

"What?" I asked. I had no idea what she was trying to suggest, but I was sure that I wasn't going to like it.

Kiara pulled to the side of the hallway.

"Kiara!" I complained as she unceremoniously shoved me behind a large fake plant.

"Shhh," she said. She pushed a couple of the plant

leaves down so she could see the hallway. "I don't want Robyn to know we're here."

"You want to spy on her?" I asked incredulously.

"It's not spying," Kiara said. Her tone of voice made it clear that she thought I was an idiot for suggesting such a thing. "We're just watching to see what's going on without interrupting them."

I shook my head but didn't complain. We still had at least twenty minutes until the movie theatre opened, and there was nothing better to do. Kiara peered through the gap in the plant again.

"They're so cute together!" She squealed. "Oh my gosh, it's too bad neither of us are dating anyone. We could do like double dates and stuff."

"She's on her first date with this girl, Kiara," I muttered. I leaned against the wall and crossed my arms. "I highly doubt she will want to go on double dates anytime soon."

"But we could do it sometime in the future," Kiara said. She glanced back at me. "You know, when I'm back from camp."

"When? We leave for school a week later."

"Yeah, so when we're back at school."

"But Robyn lives here."

Kiara's mouth gaped open. "She didn't tell you?"

"Tell me what?" I asked. I was getting a little uneasy and suddenly wishing that I had listened some of those times when Robyn was talking about her life.

"She's transferring to our university next year," Kiara said.

Oh, for goodness sake, I really cannot catch a break.

"Why?"

Kiara shrugged. "Nicer city. Better program. She didn't really like her old university much, anyway."

I sighed. Not only did I have to deal with Robyn at work, now I would have to deal with her at school — the one place that I was previously guaranteed not to see anyone from my hometown, save for Kiara.

"Hey, Harlee, look at this!" Kiara said. She was looking at Robyn and Celine again and waving her hand behind her like she was trying to tap me to get my attention but failing miserably. I moved to stand beside her and looked out. Robyn and Celine were waiting in line at the popcorn shop down the hall (how that place stayed in business beside a movie theatre, I will never understand). Celine had her arm looped around Robyn's and was laughing like Robyn had said something hilarious — I was certain her laugh had to be fake because Robyn was not a funny person. Robyn seemed to feel the same way, since she had a somewhat confused smile on her face.

Robyn was slightly taller than Celine, so she leaned down slightly as she tucked Celine's hair back behind her ear. Celine smiled widely at her, then pecked her lips. I cringed back.

"Let's go," I said. I was getting annoyed being anywhere in Robyn's vicinity.

"What?" Kiara asked. "The theatre probably won't open for a few more minutes. Why don't we wait?"

I bit my lip and took a deep breath to calm myself down. It wasn't Kiara's fault that I was annoyed right now.

"We can still get our food and drinks," I said. "Or we can go shopping for a few minutes if you want."

"But they're so cute, Harlee!" Kiara protested. I rolled my eyes.

"They're not puppies, Kiara," I said. "And it's weird to spy on them. Let's go."

Kiara sighed but dropped her hold on the plant leaves. They sprung back into place immediately, cutting off the sight of the two lovebirds.

"Fine," she said. "I want to go into Hot Topic, though."

I gratefully walked away with her.

"I don't understand why you love Hot Topic so much," I said. "It's not your style."

"Being a fangirl is my style."

Despite the joke being incredibly lame, I laughed. We spent the next twenty minutes looking around the store before we went to the movie theatre. And although I tried my best, I could not erase the image of Robyn and Celine from my mind.

❧

"I give it 3 stars," I said as we walked out of the movie theatre.

"Out of five?" Kiara asked.

"What other star rating system is there?"

"I just wanted to make sure you weren't rating it out of ten! Sometimes, you like to rate movies like that."

"But not with stars. That's always a five-level ranking."

Kiara rolled her eyes. "Sorry, I doubted your perfect five-star rating system."

I knocked my shoulder into hers. "Okay, smart ass. What did you think of the movie?"

"I give it seven balloons out of twelve," she said confidently.

"Balloons?" I cried.

"I thought you would be more caught up in the 12 point ranking system," she said with a grin.

"I can't deal with that right now," I said dramatically, placing the back of my hand against my forehead.

Kiara laughed. We pushed the heavy glass doors open and walked outside. The evening air was still pretty warm, though it was much cooler than it had been when we arrived. We both looked around for Kiara's mom's car, but it was nowhere to be seen.

Kiara was waiting for her phone to turn on again since she had completely shut it down while we were in the movies. One time in high school, her phone had rung loudly despite her putting it on silent, so now she never took chances.

"Oh, she texted me," Kiara said. She quickly read over the text. "She said she'll be here sometime before 9:15."

I checked my watch. "So we have up to twenty minutes to kill."

"Yeah," Kiara said. She put her phone back in her pocket then sat down on the curb. After a moment's hesitation, because I was wearing a nice pair of jeans and wasn't sure how I felt about sitting on the dirty ground, I joined her.

"You have plans for tomorrow?" I asked. "I was thinking we could go out for brunch or something."

Since the time we were kids, Kiara and I had had sleepovers almost every Saturday night. The tradition fell apart when we moved to residence since we were roommates, and as Kiara put it, every night was like a sleepover. Even if we hadn't been roommates, though, it felt pretty stupid to have a sleepover when we lived on the same floor. We'd been trying to revive it again since we got home. This week, I was staying over at her place because Greyson was having a sleepover with a few of his friends at our house.

"That sounds fun," Kiara said. "I thought maybe we could do something with Robyn."

I immediately groaned. "Why do you want to hang out with Robyn so much?"

"We talked about this. She's my friend." She grinned at me mischievously. "Why? Are you jealous?"

I snorted. "Jealous of what?"

"I don't know. Maybe you think I like her more than you or something."

"I'm not worried about you liking Robyn more than me," I said flatly. "I'm worried about you liking Robyn at all because it shows that you have terrible taste in friends outside of me."

Kiara laughed, then slapped a hand over her mouth.

"That's not funny," she said.

I raised my eyebrows. "Then why'd you laugh?"

"I was just laughing in surprise! I didn't expect you to say something like that."

"Expect the unexpected."

"Okay, Yoda."

"I think it's an Oscar Wilde quote, actually."

She snorted. "Of course you know that." She paused. "Anyway, we can do brunch just the two of us if you want, but I thought we could see if Robyn's free in the afternoon."

Great, we're back to Robyn.

"I just don't see why you're so insistent on hanging out with Robyn so much now when you literally hadn't spoken to her in five years before last Monday."

"I guess we just hit it off really quickly," Kiara said with a shrug. "And I won't get to see her while I'm at camp, obviously, so I want to make the most of it now."

"I don't see why you like her anyway," I muttered. I understood spending a lot of time with someone when you first become friends with them, but their friendship as a whole didn't make much sense to me.

"She's actually a really sweet person," Kiara said. "Maybe if you stopped judging her based on something she did when she was ten years old, you would see that."

"She was thirteen," I corrected, assuming she was referring to Robyn ruining my book. "And I'm certain she hasn't changed in that time."

"How could she if you never even give her a chance?" Kiara asked.

"I—"

"Oh, there's my mom," Kiara said, standing up. It was probably best that she cut me off because I had no idea what I was going to say. I stood up as well and brushed non-existent dirt off my pants.

I was a little worried Kiara was mad at me, but it didn't seem like she was because she climbed in the backseat beside me rather than calling shotgun. She always sat in the front when she was angry because it gave her an excuse not to talk.

"How was the movie, girls?" Mrs.Nichols asked.

We both filled her in, then rehashed the silly disagreement about what qualified as a proper rating system. I laughed the whole way home.

Kiara fell asleep early that night, but I stayed up to read some more. We were going to sleep in her room, but there was a heatwave going on, and it was too hot to share a bed, so we moved down to the basement where we could sleep on the couches. I took the couch that had a floor lamp right beside it, so I didn't have to leave the overhead light on to read.

Unfortunately, I was struggling to focus. I only had 100 pages left in the book, which I felt I could feasibly finish reading before going to sleep, especially since it was a Saturday night, but my mind kept drifting away from the book. I would read five pages, then realize I had no idea what was going on and have to go back to start again. Finally, I just gave up and put my book down, although I was still not tired at all.

I couldn't stop thinking about Robyn and the way she had stood with Celine. I recognized that it was completely irrational of me to be angry that Robyn had gone on a date, but I couldn't stop the feeling. I mean, who in their right mind would want to date her? She probably ruined that poor girl's night. Granted, she didn't look that upset when we saw her, but that was probably because she was trying to fake her enjoyment, so she didn't hurt Robyn's feelings. Her laugh was fake, so why couldn't all of it be fake, right?

Since I was thinking about Robyn anyway, I figured I might as well check her Goodreads. It was still at the exact same place it had been that morning, her being 67% of the way through some thriller. I refreshed the page a couple times to see if the app was just having trouble synching up, but that wasn't it. There was no way she hadn't read anything that day, even if she had been focused on her date in the evening. She was much too competitive for that. She was probably secretly reading and not marking it down so she could blindside me with her progress later.

I put a calendar notification in my phone to remind me to talk to Robyn about that. We should make a rule for the competition that we had to update our Goodreads at least once a day or every twelve hours or something so we could both keep track. For a moment, I thought about how I couldn't believe she could cheat like that, but then I realized that wasn't true — I absolutely believed that Robyn Huang would cheat to win something against me. That was exactly the kind of thing she would do.

I guess she just hadn't anticipated that I was willing to call her bluff.

12

"REMIND me why I'm coming to this again," I grumbled as we walked to the cute little pizza place Kiara had picked out for lunch. We were meeting up with Robyn there.

"Because you love me," Kiara said in a sing-song voice. "And you love pizza."

I could get pizza at home.

"You're lucky I like you so much."

We turned the corner and saw Robyn standing outside the restaurant. She was dressed in a T-shirt tucked into a skater skirt with her hair in two French braids. I hated to admit it, but she actually looked quite good.

"Hey, guys!" She said happily when we walked up. Kiara immediately went in for a hug, which Robyn eagerly returned, but I stood a good couple of feet away.

"Have you been here before?" Kiara asked. She opened the door, so we could walk inside.

"No, I haven't, but I've been meaning to try it for ages," Robyn said. I was a little surprised by her response; there were few restaurants in our town, so most people have tried all of them.

"You're going to love it," Kiara promised. "Right, Harlee?"

"Best pizza in town," I said, refusing to look at Robyn.

"I look forward to it." There was an iciness in her tone, and I could feel her eyes burning a hole in the side of my head.

"Hi there," the hostess said. "Can I help you?"

"Could we get a table for three, please?" Kiara asked.

"Of course," the hostess said. Part of me had been hoping she would say they didn't have any places today, but I supposed that was just wishful thinking. She led us over to a table with four seats. Kiara sat down first, and Robyn sat next to her. I quickly chose the spot across from Kiara so I wouldn't have to be looking at Robyn for the whole meal. "I'll give you a minute with the menus. Can I get you anything to drink in the meantime?"

"Just water is fine," I said.

"I'll take a coke," Robyn said.

"Me too," Kiara said. Of course, you'll do the same thing as Robyn.

The hostess nodded and walked off. The conversation was pretty dull until the pizza arrived. Kiara told Robyn about her camp, and Robyn said something about how she used to go to camp when she was younger. I mostly ignored them and thought about the book I was reading. I had an idea of what the plot twist was going to be, and I was very curious to see if the plot twist was right.

I didn't realize how hungry I was until the food arrived. As soon as it did, I began to eat with gusto.

"So," Kiara said a minute later. She put her elbows on the table and looked at Robyn. "How was your date last night?"

I choked on the pizza I was swallowing at that moment. Somehow, I'd completely forgotten about Robyn's date and the entire reason Kiara wanted to see Robyn today.

"Oh," Robyn said. I got a little satisfaction in seeing that she was caught off guard. "It was good."

"Just good?" Kiara asked. "Come on, give us some details!"

Robyn laughed lightly and put down the slice of pizza she'd been holding.

"What do you want to know?"

"Did you like her?" Kiara asked imploringly. "Was she nice? What did you guys do?"

"I did like her," Robyn confirmed. My nails dug into my palm. "She was lovely. Cute. We went to an Italian restaurant, over by the mall. Then we walked around for a little. Went into a bookshop and bought each other a book."

"That's adorable," Kiara said. "What book did you get her?"

"It was some science fiction novel," Robyn said. She shrugged. "And she got me a fantasy romance, so I guess she understands my personality pretty well."

Kiara's eyes flitted to me, and I wasn't surprised.

Fantasy romance was my favourite genre as well; I didn't know Robyn liked it too. Kiara probably thought that this was fantastic, now Robyn and I had common ground to discuss.

How wrong she was. Robyn liking fantasy romance effectively ruined it for me.

"Do you think you're going to go out with her again?" Kiara asked.

"I hope I will," Robyn said.

I stood abruptly.

"I'm going to the washroom," I muttered when they both looked at me wide-eyed. I walked away quickly, not wanting to hear any more of their conversation. When I got to the washroom, I wanted to splash some cold water on my face, but I didn't want to ruin my makeup (especially my eyeliner) that I'd spent a good amount of time perfecting that morning. Instead, I settled for just running my hands under cold water, which was not nearly as effective.

I paced in the small space, thankful that there was no one in there already who would probably wonder what the hell I was doing. Robyn having fun on her date shouldn't be a big deal to me. Like I'd realized the other day, if she continued going out with someone long-term, then she probably wouldn't have as much time to spend with Kiara come fall. Gosh, I couldn't believe she was transferring to our university. So Robyn having a girlfriend would be ideal if this situation came to be that. Why should that bother me?

I guess I felt bad for the girl, in the same way that I felt bad for Kiara — they only thought they liked Robyn because they didn't see the kind of person she really was. But why should I care what some random girl was doing? It wasn't like I knew her or anything.

"Get a grip, Harlee," I muttered to myself. I shook my arms to let some of my nervous energy out. Where it had come from, I couldn't tell. I took a deep breath. I had to go back out there. I had to just sit and listen to Robyn talk about her date or whatever other shit she would talk about for the next hour, then I could go home and forget all about this. I never had to think about *Robyn's fucking date and fucking perfect girl* ever again.

❧

The lunch ended up going for longer than I'd anticipated. I thought it would be an hour, maybe an hour and a half at most, but Kiara managed to drag it out to over two hours.

"So, I guess you haven't finished any books today, huh?" Kiara asked when we got back to her house. She tossed her purse on the couch and turned to me, hooking her thumbs in her belt loops. Then she said teasingly, "How ever will you win the competition now?"

I just glared at her. First, she made me listen to Robyn ramble for hours about the girl she was seeing and now she was reminding me that I was slowly falling behind on the competition?

"Oh, lighten up," Kiara said, rolling her eyes. She spun on her heel and went into the kitchen. "You used to be so much more fun!"

"Hey!" I argued. I trailed after her and sat at the island counter. "I am fun!"

"Not right now, you're not," Kiara said.

"I'm sorry you feel that way," I muttered. I pulled my phone out and checked Goodreads. I was satisfied to see that she had updated her progress on the book she was reading. At lunch, I'd brought up the rule of updating Goodreads at least once a day, and she had agreed.

Since I had finished a book yesterday and Robyn hadn't, I was one book ahead of her. If I finished the book I was currently reading by that night and Robyn didn't do anything, then I would be two books ahead, which was my ideal situation.

"I think I'm going to try to stay two books ahead of Robyn for the rest of the summer," I said. "To make sure I win."

"Remember, this is just some stupid competition," Kiara said.

"It's not stupid," I said. "I *need* to beat Robyn. She still thinks she had the last win by destroying my book."

Kiara rubbed her temples. "I still don't understand why you're keeping score of that."

"I'm keeping score because she's keeping score."

"*If* she's keeping score — and I really don't think she is — it's probably because you're keeping score," Kiara said. "Do you see where the problem is?"

"No," I said simply. I stood up. "I need to go. I have some stuff to finish tonight. I'll see you tomorrow?"

Kiara nodded. It went without saying that she

would meet me after work since that had obviously become our ritual over the last week.

On my way home, I brainstormed some ways I could keep ahead of Robyn in the competition. Reading during my breaks and before work were obvious ways, but I was sure to burn out quickly if I did that for too long. I really needed those breaks when I was working. Of course, once Kiara left for camp next week, I would have a lot more time after work to get some reading done, so that would help. I couldn't be sure if it would be enough, though. Considering how often Kiara had invited Robyn to hang out with us, Robyn would probably have the same thing.

When I got home, I went straight upstairs, still thinking about this issue. The solution hit me in the face when I was picking out my books to read for the next week. Almost everything that I had recently bought and wanted to read were really long books, mostly fantasy books that took a couple of days to finish reading. If I switched to reading shorter books for the summer, it would take much less time for me to finish each book. In fact, if I focused primarily on classics and middle-grade books, I could probably double my output each week. I could even throw in a few historical romances, which I could read quickly, despite being longer than some of the other books.

I went to text Kiara about my plan, then faltered. She would probably just say that I should keep reading what I wanted instead of focusing on the competition — she just didn't understand. I put my phone down slowly.

It was better to keep this to myself for the time being.

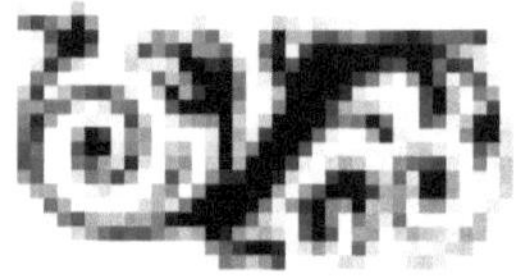

The next night, I checked Goodreads again when I got home. I was satisfied to see that I was still two books ahead. I would probably be finishing another book that night as well, so I was doing just fine. Unless Robyn was holding back on updating her Goodreads. At lunch the other day, she said she hadn't had the time to read for a few days, but I had no way of knowing whether that was true. For all I knew, she was lying to throw me off her trail. Unfortunately, I had no way of knowing for certain, so the best thing I could do was just read as fast as possible.

I did finish the book I had started the night before, some historical romance set in the 1800s, but like the other night at Kiara's house, I really struggled to concentrate on it. I couldn't stop thinking about Robyn and her stupid fucking date. Who the hell was Robyn to get to go out with a nice girl? I hadn't had a date in months, and here she was going out with a girl who, by her standards at least, was perfect.

I didn't want to be one of those girls acting like *woe is me, I will never be in a relationship*, but that was how I was feeling at that moment. First, April and Bree got together. Then, Robyn seemed to find somebody. Who was next? Was Kiara going to leave single and come back with a significant other, leaving me to wallow alone for the rest of my life?

I sighed. *Reading all these romance books is getting to me. I should switch to middle grade or something.* I picked up another book from the pile on my nightstand, this one being a Nancy Drew book that I could probably finish by morning.

Perfect. This one won't have any romance in it — and more importantly, it will have nothing that will remind me of Robyn.

13

Work on Tuesday was actually pretty fun, despite Robyn being there. I was feeling pretty good about everything, especially since I was going to Kiara's place after work, and I knew for a fact that it would just be the two of us.

Unfortunately, my fantastic mood was quickly ruined when I opened Goodreads. On my homepage, the first notification was that Robyn had finished a book and rated it four stars. That was all well and good until I scrolled down and saw that she had finished four books. Overnight. Which easily put her in the lead.

I was standing just outside the store, having just finished my shift. I looked around the parking lot for Robyn and spotted her walking towards the bike rack.

"Hey!" I yelled, storming after her. Robyn continued unlocking her bike without a care in the world, not even bothering to look over at me. When I got a little closer, I repeated myself in a louder voice. She finally turned toward me, looking exasperated.

"What do you want, Harlee?" She asked. I held up my phone, her Goodreads page still open.

"What's this?" I demanded.

She raised an eyebrow. "My Goodreads page?"

I rolled my eyes. "I know that."

"Then why are you asking me?" She asked. She turned around again. "Why are you looking at it, anyway? You stalking me or something?"

"No, I'm stalking you," I said, though I didn't sound as laid back as I would have liked. "I was just checking your Goodreads to see how you were doing in the competition."

"Right," Robyn said. She put her small bag in her bike's basket. "So, why are you following me out here, then?"

I crossed my arms. You're the one in the right here. Don't let her get you.

"You're cheating in the competition," I said.

"I am?" She asked. I nodded stiffly. "Well, that's news to me."

"It shouldn't be." I scrolled down the page to show her the activity feed then held the phone out to her again. "You added four books last night."

She barely glanced at the screen.

"Yeah," she said. "So?"

"So, there is no way you read four books in a night!" I snapped. She didn't even bat an eye, which only made me angrier.

"You don't know that."

"It's impossible that you read that fast, Robyn."

"Once again, you don't know that. Maybe I'm a speed reader."

"Right, that explains why you didn't read for five days straight, then read four books in one night."

"I needed to catch up."

"Or you read all those books and didn't log them right away, even though that goes against my agreement."

"You can't prove that."

"They're four long fantasy books! There's no way you read them that quickly!" I knew she was just trying to rile me up, and I wanted to stay calm and collected like her, but I just couldn't do it. She got on my nerves way too much. "Especially at a time when you should have been sleeping."

"Should have been sleeping?" She asked. "Who are you, my mom?"

"You know what I meant," I said. I gestured my hand uselessly. "Most people sleep at night."

"Maybe I'm not most people, then."

"When do you sleep, then? You work all day."

"I only work until four most days," she said. "Maybe I sleep right when I get home."

"You go out with Kiara and me after work most days."

"But not yesterday."

I huffed. "You were active on Instagram until eleven o'clock last night. That means you weren't sleeping in that time."

"So you are stalking me," Robyn said. She slipped

her hands in her back pocket and tilted her head slightly as she looked at me. "I gotta say, I'm flattered, Harlee."

"Don't be weird," I muttered.

She placed a hand on her chest. "Sorry, you're calling me weird? You're the one who obsessively checks my Goodreads to see what I'm up to."

"I need to know what you're doing for the competition!"

"I'm a part of the competition too, and I don't check your Goodreads."

"And that's why you're going to lose," I said icily. She narrowed her eyes.

"I can read four books in a night," she said. "And the fact that you're so angry about it means that you can't. So I wouldn't be so sure about your possible victory if I was you."

I shook my head, suddenly remembering why I was there. I'd gotten side-tracked.

"You were cheating," I said, "and I'm not going to do this competition if you cheat."

"Like I said," Robyn said in an impatient tone, "you can't prove that I was cheating. And pulling out of the competition means I win."

"You didn't win anything," I snapped. "Just update your Goodreads more frequently."

She pointed a finger at me. "You said once a day. I did update once a day."

"You did not read four books in one day!"

"Maybe I did! I could be a vampire who doesn't need to sleep, you don't know."

Despite my anger at her, I snorted at that comment. I immediately wanted to take it back when she smiled at me triumphantly.

"Now, if you'll excuse me," she said, pulling her bike off the rack, "I need to get going. Many more books to read. People to kill. You know, the usual."

"I hate you," I muttered because I couldn't admit that her jokes were funny. Robyn Huang was not a funny person — she just had occasional good one-liners.

"Back at you!" She said happily as she kicked off. "See you in the morning."

"See you," I said quietly. I pulled my own bike out too but waited a couple minutes before I left as well. Assuming she was going to her house, we were going in the same direction, and I didn't want to end up stuck at a stoplight with her or something.

When I got to Kiara's house, I told her (well, more like ranted at her) about the whole situation. Unfortunately, we have the same sense of humour, so she thought Robyn's vampire joke was funny and then began to theorize about whether it was true.

"She is not a vampire!" I insisted, pacing back and forth in her basement.

"That's what she wants you to think," Kiara said in a conspiring tone. "But how can we know for certain?"

I paused in my step. "Well, I guess the only way to know for sure is to stab her with a wooden stake. But I'm guessing you're against that idea."

"Well..." Kiara said. For a moment, I actually thought she was going to say we should do it. Then she shook her head and said, "No. No, we can't do that."

"As fun as it would be," I murmured.

"What?"

"Nothing."

$\mathfrak{H}$ 14 $\mathfrak{R}$

"Harlee, what are you doing?" Bree asked during our call the next day.

"Hm?" I asked, not looking up from the page I was reading. The main characters were just leaving on the quest, and I was getting a rising sense of dread that something would go wrong.

"What are you doing?" Bree repeated.

"Oh. Reading." I turned the page. My eyes jumped down the end of the page, completely spoiling the end of the chapter for me. I groaned and slammed the book shut, needing a moment to deal with that before I could continue going.

"You good?" April asked.

"Fine," I said tightly. I put my book aside and moved my laptop closer to me so I could see them better. "How are you guys?"

"If you listened during the call, then you would probably know," Kiara pointed out.

"I'm a busy person," I said. "I need to multi-task."

"You're so desperate to get reading done that you can't spare any time to talk to your friends?" Bree asked. She tried to mask it like she was joking, but I could hear the hurt in her voice.

"Sorry," I said honestly. "I didn't mean to ignore you. I just need to catch up in this reading competition."

"Reading competition?" Elyssa asked, tilting her head.

"Did I not tell you about it?"

April, Bree, and Elyssa all shook their heads.

"Oh," I said. "Well, I work with this girl, Robyn."

"Oh, is it the same girl Kiara is friends with?" Bree asked.

"Yes, but I'm not friends with her. She's my sworn enemy."

"That's a little dramatic, Harlee," Kiara said.

I lifted my chin. "No, it's not. She is my sworn enemy and has been since we were six years old, and she married Jackie Thomas on the playground even though she knew I liked her."

"That's where this rivalry started?" Kiara asked in disbelief.

Honestly, it was hard to pinpoint the exact moment Robyn and I had started hating each other. There were many factors leading into it, most of which involving us being on different sports teams, but I liked to point to that day in first grade as the beginning of everything.

"Yes," I said. "Anyway, we're having this competition to see who can read more books by the end of the summer, and she suddenly jumped ahead, so now I have to catch up."

"You're having a reading competition with your sworn enemy," Bree said.

"Yes."

She shook her head. "Only you, Harlee. Only you."

15

"I WAS THINKING we could get pizza again today," Kiara said when we met up after work on Thursday. "I mean, we can do something else first if you want since it's not really dinner time yet, but after that, I want to get pizza."

"Okay," I said with a shrug. It didn't make much of a difference to me what we did.

"How was work?"

"It was fine. Had a couple annoying customers, but that's just a day in the life working in retail."

Kiara nodded and said, "Good, good."

I frowned. Annoying customers was good? I looked at her. She was staring off into the distance, seeming lost in thought.

"You okay?" I asked.

Her head snapped in my direction. "Hm?"

"You okay?" I repeated. I gestured vaguely at her. "You seem... distracted."

"Oh. Oh yeah, I'm fine. Just a lot on my mind."

"Something you want to talk about?"

"No, no." She picked at her fingernails a bit. "So, where did we land on the pizza thing? Now or later?"

"We could go now if you want," I said. "I am a little hungry."

"Okay," Kiara said. She was being oddly tame in her reaction, which only made me that much more concerned. Kiara was not a calm person, especially not when it came to pizza.

We sat on a different side of the restaurant than we had the other day with Robyn, at a table for two. After the day I had, I was really tempted to order a glass of wine, but it was only four o'clock in the afternoon, which felt a little too early.

"I started a new show last night," Kiara said as we waited for the food.

"Oh?" I asked. "Which one?"

We often watched the same shows at the same time so we could talk about them.

"It's..." She trailed off in thought then shook her head. "I forget the name. I never heard of it before; it just showed up on my recommended list."

"Send it to me later," I said. "I'll check it out."

She nodded. I expected her to tell me what the show was about, but she was looking away from me, lost in thought yet again. We sat in silence until the waitress dropped off our food.

"Thank you," I said. I went to start then noticed Kiara hadn't even noticed the pizza sitting in front of her. I snapped my fingers a couple times in front of her face. "Kiara!"

She jerked. "What? Oh, sorry, zoned out."

"Yeah, I noticed," I said. "You sure everything is okay?"

"Yeah, yeah." She picked up a slice and nibbled on her pizza for a couple minutes, still very distracted. I began to wonder why she even asked me to meet up with her if she had so much to think about. After five minutes of this, and not even finishing a single slice, she put her food down and looked at me seriously.

"I've been thinking," she said.

"Thinking is good," I said. I was a little worried given how serious she looked, and I wanted to lighten the mood. The corner of her mouth raised in what could be perceived as a smile, though I think it was more a smile of pity than of amusement.

Kiara took a deep breath. "I'm sorry for trying to push you to be friends with Robyn. I can see now that there's a lot more to the situation that I didn't understand, and I shouldn't have pushed the issue so hard. And I'm sorry for how that affected our friendship too."

I stared at her for a moment, a little taken aback. I hadn't been expecting an apology from her today, especially not about that. Over the past week and a half, she had made it pretty clear to me that she was going to be friends with Robyn, whether I liked it or not.

"Thank you," I said slowly. That was the correct response, right? She was listening to my feelings and validating them, which was good.

"You don't..." she swallowed. "You don't have to thank me for apologizing. I mean, I was the one in the wrong."

"But I'm grateful," I said. "Not many people are willing to swallow their pride and say sorry."

I'm definitely one of those people.

"Right," Kiara said. She smiled. "Anyway, onto less depressing subjects. What should we do on Saturday?"

I could tell she didn't want to dwell on this subject, so I let her seamlessly change the conversation. In my mind, though, I was still running over what she said. The tension between us definitely hadn't been all on her by any means. She was right in what she said the week before about me obsessing over hating Robyn. I needed to work on allowing my friendship with Kiara to come before my rivalry with Robyn. And maybe I was being too hard on Robyn — only a little too hard, mind you. If it would make Kiara happy, I could make more of an effort.

All in all, I was just happy to be on good terms with my best friend before she left for the summer.

16

I had Friday off, so I went over to Kiara's in the morning.

"I changed my mind," Kiara said as soon as I walked into her room. I paused mid-stride.

"About me coming over?" I asked slowly since that was the only thing topical at that moment.

"About our plans for tonight," Kiara clarified. She sat on the edge of her bed. "I know we were planning to go clubbing, but I don't really feel like it anymore. I was thinking something more simple, like dinner and drinks."

"I'm fine with that," I said.

"Really?" She asked with immense relief.

"Why wouldn't I be?" I asked. "We can do whatever you want."

Tomorrow was Kiara's last night in town before leaving for camp, but her parents wanted her to be home for dinner, so we were celebrating tonight instead.

"Thank you!" Kiara said. She jumped up and hugged me. I stumbled back a little in surprise but let her hold on for another moment before I stepped away. Kiara was a big hugger, and I was not, so that was my compromise.

"So, dinner?" I asked as I pulled away.

"Right!" Kiara said. She laid down on her bed again and opened her laptop. I laid down beside her so I could see the screen as well. "I wasn't sure what you would want. I know we go to Italian places like every day, so I thought maybe we should try something different."

"Okay," I said. We had gone to an Italian place twice in the last week, so that would make sense to do.

"But then, I was like, why mess with something we know we like," she continued. "Which leaves me here... with no ideas."

"To be fair, there aren't a lot of restaurants in the area," I said. "We might have to settle for something."

"Yeah, I know," Kiara sighed. "We could take an uber a little out of town."

"A little out of town is still a pretty long way," I said. She knew that, of course. This was the same conversation we had any time we wanted to go somewhere.

"There's that newer place out by the river," Kiara said. She looked up restaurants near us in Google Maps. "There. It's also an Italian place but a different one than we normally go to."

"I'm fine with it if you are," I said.

"Okay, let's do it. I'll call and make a reservation," Kiara said. She threw her laptop down on the bed and walked across the room to her phone. I sat up, my hair falling against my back.

"And by that, do you mean I will call and make a reservation?" I asked. I was almost always the one to do stuff like that for our friend group. Bree sometimes joked that I was the "mom friend," but I didn't think that was an accurate representation since I definitely wasn't the most responsible of the group. I was just the most confident in social situations like calling a restaurant.

"If you don't mind," Kiara said in a sweet voice.

"Yeah, I don't care." I grabbed my phone and started to type in the number that was listed on the website. Before I could press the call button, though, I asked, "Do you want to invite anyone else?"

Kiara's eyebrows furrowed. "Somebody else? Like who?"

I shrugged, although I was pretty sure we both knew who I had in mind. We didn't have many friends in East Port, so there was really only one option, and I didn't want to have to be the one to say it.

"Anyone you want," I said slowly. Kiara just stared at me. I sighed. "Do you want to invite Robyn?"

Her mouth fell open slightly, and she seemed genuinely surprised. Had she really not understood what I was alluding to?

"Would you mind?" She asked. My first instinct was to say yes, I did mind, and we should just forget the whole thing. But I didn't want her to feel like she couldn't invite her friend because of me. I could suck it up and act friendly toward Robyn for one night.

"No," I said with a forced smile. "I don't mind."

"Thank you, Harlee!" She said. "I'll call her right now and ask if she's free."

"Is she not working now?" I asked.

"Guess we'll find out," Kiara said. She grabbed her phone and ran into the hallway to make the call. I frowned. She didn't usually leave the room to make phone calls. I felt a little pang in my heart, like I thought she was going to gossip about me with Robyn on the call or something. Of course, Kiara wouldn't do that because she wasn't like that, but I couldn't shake off the worry. The insecurity built with every minute that she was out in the hallway, but she finally returned with a large smile. "She is free! So we'll do a table for three."

I nodded and picked up my phone again, trying to push all my previous feelings aside. The phone only rang a couple times before somebody answered. I quickly made a reservation for the three of us, thankful that they accepted same-day reservations because I knew there were definitely many restaurants that didn't.

"We're all set," I said after I hung up. "What should we do now?"

"Let's go down to the hot tub," Kiara said.

I laughed. When in doubt, that was always our go-to activity.

"Sounds good."

Kiara and I got to the restaurant earlier than Robyn, so we waited at the table for her. We sat in silence for the most part while we waited since we had spent the whole day together, and there's only so much you can talk about.

Kiara and I were sitting across from each other, so I could see the entrance to the restaurant, and she couldn't. I kept an eye out for Robyn while also looking around the room. Remembering the promise I made to myself the other day, I decided I would make an actual effort to get along with Robyn at dinner. Well, maybe not actually getting along with her since that was near impossible, but I would listen when she was talking and try to engage in the conversation.

"There's Robyn," I said after we'd been sitting there for a little under ten minutes. The hostess led her over, and Robyn sat in the chair next to Kiara.

"Sorry I'm late," she said. She brushed some of her hair out of her face. She was dressed in a nice burgundy off-the-shoulder dress and had her black hair curled. I guess she had looked up the restaurant and decided to dress the part, like Kiara and I.

"You will not believe the day I had today," Robyn said. "The store was crazy. You're lucky you weren't working today, Harlee."

A retort was on my lips, but I bit it back. If Kiara could be the bigger person, then so could I.

"What happened?" I asked politely. Robyn looked at me a little weirdly, but she launched into her story about the day anyway. I did listen to her the whole time, though I found myself having to hold back most of my comments since they would probably be a little too snarky to say. I did have to admit, Robyn was a pretty good storyteller, and I could see why Kiara liked to talk to her. She had a way of embellishing her stories just enough that they seemed funnier than they necessarily should have, without it coming off as over the top.

Our conversation continued in the same vein throughout dinner. Robyn shared many stories about her time working at the bookstore, and I laughed along more than I expected.

"Sounds like you're in for one hell of a summer if your experiences are anything like Robyn's," Kiara said to me after Robyn finished telling us the story of a guy who tried to deal some more by shoving them up his shirt.

"Hopefully, this summer isn't too crazy," Robyn said. "I could do with a calmer season, after everything from the spring."

"That's what Harlee's looking for, too," Kiara said.

I tried to gesture for her to stop talking, but it was hard to subtly do that with Robyn sitting right there. I understood that she probably thought this was all fine to say, but I didn't want her making comparisons between Robyn and me, and I definitely didn't want Robyn to know what I wanted from the summer because she would do everything she could to ruin those plans.

"Oh yeah?" Robyn asked. She looked at me, and I shrugged like *yeah, I guess, but it doesn't really matter*. "I would have expected you to be more of a looking-for-adventure type."

"I'm full of surprises," I said, rubbing a hand over my eyes.

Our waitress, Lily, walked over a moment later.

"Can I get you ladies anything else?" She asked.

"Could we get a dessert menu?" Kiara asked.

"Yes, of course," she said. "I'll be right back with that."

"I don't know why you even bother to ask for the dessert menu," I said. "You always get the same thing every time."

"I do not!" Kiara said.

I raised my eyebrows. "Tiramisu?"

"Sometimes I branch out," she muttered.

Robyn laughed. "Don't worry, Kiara, I always get the same dessert every time."

Kiara looked at me like, *See? I'm not the only one!* As if using Robyn as an example was the way to convince that something was normal and acceptable.

"Here you are," our waitress said, handing out the menus. "I'll give you a minute with those."

"Prove it," I said to Kiara.

"What?" She asked.

"Prove you branch out. Get something other than tiramisu."

"I will," she said hotly, sending a glare in my direction. Then, she looked over the menu quickly and tried to read off the names of a few items that she might get instead. I was not an expert in Italian by any means, but even I could tell that she completely butchered the pronunciation of every single word.

"I don't think that was quite right, Kiara," I said, trying to hold back my laughter.

"You did then," Kiara said. She leaned back and crossed her arms. "Go on."

"I didn't say that I could do any better," I said.

Robyn grinned. "Did either of you take Italian class in high school?" She asked.

Kiara and I both shook our heads.

"I was going to, but my cousin convinced me not to," Kiara said. "She said the Italian teacher was terrible."

Her cousins lived in the same town as us, though they were a few years older. They warned her about which classes she absolutely should or shouldn't take when we got to choose our electives in high school.

"Oh, she absolutely was," Robyn said. She grimaced. "I'm not sure I learned a single thing in that class except how to say 'shut up' and 'I hate children'."

"She was that bad?" I asked. I took a sip of my drink.

"Awful!" Robyn said. "In fact, she used to put her head down on her desk and say how much she hated her job and our class."

"That's a quality you want in a teacher," I said drily.

"I know, right?" Robyn did a thumbs up. "Real inspiring."

"If you weren't turned away from being a teacher before, you are now," Kiara said. She took a sip of wine.

"Do you ever feel like that when you're at camp?" I

asked her. "I would assume being a counsellor is even worse than a teacher because you're stuck with those kids twenty-four seven."

Kiara tilted her head from side to side like she was saying it was so-so.

"It depends," she said. "Generally, kids want to be at camp, unlike school. And you're only stuck with them for two weeks instead of ten months."

Lily reappeared by our table. "Have you had enough time with the menus?"

"Yes, I'll get the tiramisu, please," Kiara said. I snorted but didn't say anything.

"I'll get whichever gelato you recommend," Robyn said. I stared at her, though she wasn't looking at me. Kiara hadn't told her to say that, had she? It seemed unlikely that Robyn would get the exact same dessert that I always got, though I didn't see any reason why she would pretend to.

I realized a moment too late that Lily was looking to me now, wondering what I wanted.

"Oh, um, I'll have the same, please," I said.

Lily nodded. "It will be ready soon." She walked off.

I cleared my throat, not wanting to dwell on the fact that Robyn and I liked the same dessert. I shouldn't have found it as weird as I did, but as it was, I wanted to get the conversation back to what it was before as soon as possible.

"So, Kiara," I said. I took a moment to remember what she was saying before we had ordered dessert. "When do you not like working at camp?"

Kiara frowned in thought, but a moment later, she seemed to remember the conversation as well. "Oh, right! Well, if you get a bad cabin, then everything kind of sucks. There have definitely been times that I questioned whether it was worth the pay to have to deal with some of those kids."

"Oh yeah, camp pay is awful," Robyn said.

"It's peanuts," Kiara said. "In theory, it's because they're providing food and board, but you're also working pretty much around the clock, so that's not my favourite argument."

"They capitalize on people wanting to continue to have the camp experience," I said. "You age out of being able to be a camper, so you become a counsellor instead."

"Exactly," Kiara said. "I guess they got me with that trick."

"Do you think you'll keep working there after this year?" Robyn asked.

Kiara shrugged. "Maybe. I'll have to see whether I can keep this supervisor position for another year."

"Are you going to keep working at the bookstore?" I asked Robyn. She said she'd been working there for many years already, so she obviously liked the job, but from what I'd seen in my couple of weeks working there, it was not a place people worked at for very long.

"I've always imagined myself doing it for the rest of my undergrad," Robyn said. "I guess it would be smarter to try to find an internship or something during the summers, though."

"What's your major again?" Kiara asked.

"Business," Robyn said. "Typical and boring, I know."

"I don't think it's boring," I said.

She looked at me dubiously. "No?"

I shook my head. "I don't think any major is boring. It's what you do with it that is interesting."

"So... you think I'm going to work a boring job?" Robyn asked slowly.

"That's one interpretation," I said neutrally. "On the other hand, though, I think there are many interesting things you could do with a business degree. An obvious one being that you start your own business."

Robyn laughed and shook her head. "No, I'm not like that."

"Not like what?" I asked. "An entrepreneur?"

"Yeah," Robyn said. "I'm not creative or smart enough to create my own business."

"Sure, you are," Kiara said. Kiara strongly believed that everyone could do anything they wanted, so long as they put their mind to it.

"I don't have any ideas of a business I could run," Robyn said.

"A bookstore," I said immediately.

She stared at me. I could almost see the gears turning in her head. "What?"

"You could run a bookstore. You've worked at one for so long, you must know a good amount of how it works."

"I know how to be a salesperson in a bookstore," she said. "Not how to run one."

"So learn," I said. "You could even ask Tracy to

help you. At the very least, she could point you in the right direction."

"She's only the manager, not the store owner," Robyn said. The store we worked for was a small chain, so she was right, but I still thought my point stood. "And I'm not sure she's really looking to help me leave my job."

"She's delusional if she thinks you're going to work there long-term. It's a minimum wage job. They're designed to have frequent turnover." It occurred to me that she hadn't really asked for my opinion on what she should do with her degree, and I was forcing this idea in her face, so I back-pedalled a little. "Whatever, it's up to you. It's just an option for you to consider."

"I'll keep it in mind," she said. She took another sip of her drink, this time staring at me over the rim. My heart skipped a beat — which was completely unrelated, mind you — and I quickly tore my eyes away.

"Here is your dessert," Lily said. She put the tiramisu in front of Kiara and gave Robyn and me each a bowl of gelato. "The gelato flavour of the week is pistachio. Please enjoy and let me know if you want anything else."

"Thank you," we all said.

"Here's what I don't understand about ordering just whichever flavour they recommend," Kiara said. "What if you don't like it? Like what if they bring you the most god-awful flavour gelato you've ever tried? You can't send it back because it's what you ordered."

"I don't think I've ever tried a gelato flavour I didn't like," I said.

"Same here," Robyn said. "It takes a lot to faze me."

Kiara didn't seem convinced by our answers, but she let it go.

"It worked out really well this time," I said after I had a bite of the gelato. "Pistachio is an amazing flavour."

"It's in my top ten," Robyn agreed.

"What are the other nine?" I asked.

She looked at me for a moment.

"I can't reveal all my secrets at once," she said. "I guess you'll just have to find out with time."

That's a long way of saying you don't want me to know anything about you. I didn't particularly care, anyway. I mostly just asked to be polite. Okay, maybe I was a little interested, but only a little and only because gelato was involved. But it seemed I would never find out the other flavours because once Kiara left on Sunday, Robyn and I wouldn't have to speak outside of work again.

We stayed at the restaurant for a little while after that, having some drinks and just chatting. Even though I was used to Kiara leaving for the whole summer every year, my heart ached as the night went on, and I realized I was barely going to see her for the next two months. That summer would probably be the worst of any in my life so far since I didn't know anyone else in town. Everybody I used to be friends with were strangers now, and I wouldn't know where to find them if I tried.

I supposed it could be worse — at least I had the competition to keep me company.

As per usual, the house was dark when I came inside, though this time it was because the rest of my family was asleep, rather than out. I did my best to be quiet as I walked (or more like stumbled) inside the house. I really thought I was a heavyweight, but given how few drinks I had, that didn't seem to be the case.

I kicked off my shoes as soon as I walked inside, which made it marginally easier to get upstairs. Then I did a pretty half-assed job of my nighttime routine and laid down in bed. I slammed my hand around my nightstand to turn off my lamp, and when my hand collided with my book.

That was my reminder that I hadn't read anything all day. Granted, my day had been pretty busy, but still, if I didn't read anything, then it would be the first day that I hadn't done anything to help me win this competition. And sure, I was drunk and tired, but that shouldn't stop me from reaching my goals, right? I looked for differences between Robyn and me wherever I could since our parents used to compare us so much when we were younger, and this was yet another area in which we differed: when I committed to something, I did everything in my power to follow through on it.

Yawning all the way through, I read 50 pages of my book before falling asleep with it on my chest. And when I tried to pick up where I left off the following day but had no idea what was going on, I told myself that was because it was a confusing book and not because reading when you're drunk is a really stupid idea.

17

KIARA LEFT ON SUNDAY MORNING. I went to say goodbye to her and make sure that she actually had everything she needed to survive the next two months after all her packing and unpacking. Then I went back to my house and immediately started reading, because what the hell else was I going to do?

Like I anticipated, Robyn and I barely spoke after Kiara left. We didn't even need to speak at work most of the time, so I barely said three words to her during the whole first week. With all my newfound spare time, I turned to reading constantly. Apparently, Robyn didn't do the same because when I checked Goodreads during my break on Wednesday morning, I was the furthest ahead I had been thus far in the competition.

As soon as my break was over, I went to find Robyn.

"Hey," I said, popping beside her. She barely

spared me a glance before she went back to stocking the shelves.

"Hey," she said simply.

"Guess what?" I was oddly giddy that day and actively trying to stop myself from showing it in my body language. Robyn didn't respond beyond glancing at me quickly again, so I continued. "I just check Goodreads, and I'm ten books ahead of you."

Robyn slammed a book down a little too hard, but that was the only indication she made that she heard me. She continued doing her work for another minute in silence. I wasn't sure if I should walk away, but I was honestly hoping for a little bit more of a reaction from her, so I cleared my throat.

"Did you hear me?" I asked when she still didn't react. "There's no way you're going to catch up. I'm going to win."

"Congratulations," Robyn said drily. She walked away. I stared after her, unsure of what to do. In theory, that interaction was the best I could hope for with Robyn — she didn't insult me, and she didn't hang around to chat — but I oddly felt like something was missing. Why didn't she care that I was winning? Did she not want to do the competition anymore? More importantly, why did I care? If she quit the competition, then I won by default, which should be fine by all means. But, for some reason, I didn't want the competition to end like that.

"What's wrong, Harlee?" Bree asked on our weekly call. "You miss Kiara?"

"Why do you think something's wrong?" I asked.

"I don't know. You look upset," Bree said.

"Oh." My face was usually pretty neutral, so I didn't see how she determined that.

"So, what is it?" April asked. She looked a little concerned now, as well. As concerned as April could look, at least.

"It's nothing," I said. "I'm just... You remember that reading competition I'm doing?"

"The one with your sworn enemy?" Bree asked.

"Yes," I said, ignoring the teasing in her voice. "I'm doing really well in it right now, but it seems like she doesn't even care."

"You're sad that your enemy doesn't care that you're reading more books than her?" April asked slowly.

"Well, it sounds stupid if you say it like that," I muttered. I played with the ends of my hair to avoid looking at them.

"Nobody's saying it's stupid," Elyssa said quickly. "We just want to make sure we understand."

"Yeah," Bree said agreeably. "Have you talked to the girl about it?"

"I tried to tell her that I was ahead in the competition today, but she didn't react at all," I said.

"Right," Elyssa said. "And it's no fun winning at a competition if the person you beat doesn't care."

"Exactly!" I shocked myself with how enthusiastic my voice was. In a more mellow tone, I said, "But I can't force her to care about the competition."

"Maybe the way to make her care is to spend time with her," Bree said.

I frowned. "What difference would that make?"

"Well, she only became indifferent once Kiara left, right?" Bree asked.

"I guess so. She tried to act like she didn't care before, too, but she was at least trying to keep up in the competition."

"Maybe that's because when Kiara was here, you two were forced to see each other. She had to care about the competition because she couldn't stand to be near you if she was losing."

"So, what do I do?" I asked. "You want me to willingly spend time with her?"

"You can do whatever you want," Elyssa said. "But the competition will probably be more interesting if you two are talking."

"Pretty much, we're saying you need to spend time with your enemy so you can rub it in her face that you're better than her," April said.

I thought about it for a second. "Yeah. I guess that makes sense."

❦   18   ❦

THERE WAS a special book signing event at the store on Friday night, so Robyn and I both ended up working the evening shift to help out with it. The whole event was over by eight o'clock, but we had to stay an hour past that to clean up.

When Tracy said we could leave, Robyn immediately went to grab her stuff, but I stayed where I was behind the counter, lost in thought. My friends' words from the other night were ringing in my mind, as they had been for the past day and a half.

I was upset that Robyn didn't want to talk to me, and the only way to remedy that was to ask her to hang out with me outside of work.

Since it was Friday night, it was the perfect occasion. Assuming she didn't have plans and she did want to go out, we could go get drinks or something tonight. Otherwise, we could go sometime this weekend. And if she said no, then I had the whole weekend to figure out what to do next.

I have nothing to lose, I told myself. Well, besides my dignity. Because if she says no, that will be mortifying. But other than that, nothing to lose!

I wasn't the best at giving pep talks, especially to myself.

Robyn walked out of the backroom. She wasn't walking particularly fast, but she was coming in my direction, so I only had a minute or two to make a decision about what I was going to do. I wasn't one to back down from a challenge, but I wasn't sure the possible consequences of this were worth the potential positive outcome.

She was walking by the counter. Three steps away from the door. Two. One.

"Hey," I said. She paused with her hand on the door and looked back at me. Her long braid swung as she did so. I stared at her blankly, suddenly forgetting what I was going to say.

"What?" She asked.

"Um..." I probably should have thought through what I was going to say before this. Wait, I did think of how I was going to ask her. Why couldn't I remember the speech I had prepared?

"Is everything all right?" She asked, her face twisted in confusion. She took a step toward the counter. "Did I forget something?"

"No," I said. I cleared my throat. "No, nothing like that."

Robyn's eyebrows pulled together.

"Are you okay?"

At other times, I probably would have laughed at the fact that Robyn Huang was asking if I was okay. I would have made fun of her for acting like she cared. But I was so distracted by my thoughts that I barely even registered her words.

"I was just thinking..." I found myself at a rare loss of words. I was used to being so calm and collected that I wasn't quite sure how to deal with it. "That is... I mean..."

Robyn took another step toward me. Even though there was still a counter between us, I took a step back. I looked away from her, hoping that would stop her from seeing the nervousness on my face.

"I was wondering if you wanted to go out for a drink," I said quickly. "Today or... or whenever."

Robyn didn't respond. My heart was pounding in my chest. Why the hell was I so nervous about this? What did I care what Robyn thought of me? It was no big deal, any of this. *Oh god, why isn't she responding? I shouldn't have said that anything. I should have—*

"Sure."

My head whipped up so fast it hurt my neck.

"Sure?" I asked. She shifted her bag on her shoulder and nodded.

"Yeah. I'm free now if you want."

"Kiara won't be there," I blurted out. "She left for camp a couple weeks ago."

"I know," Robyn said.

"Oh. Right." Of course, she knew that. I was such an idiot.

"So..." Robyn said. "Do you want to get drinks now?"

"Uh... yes," I said, but I didn't move. She raised her eyebrows. "Just let me grab my stuff."

"Okay."

I walked to the backroom, feeling her eyes burning a hole in the back of my head as I did so. She was probably confused by my actions. I would be if I was her.

I tried to get my stuff together quickly, not wanting to leave her waiting for too long or give myself too much time to think about what I was doing. I was in and out in less than a minute, then we went outside.

"Where's your bike?" I asked as I unlocked my bike. It was the only one in the rack.

"I didn't bring it," Robyn said.

"Did you drive?" I asked as I pulled my bike out and turned to her. Robyn blushed slightly.

"Ah... no."

"How did you get here, then?" I asked slowly.

"I rollerbladed," she said. I pressed my lips together, trying to hold back laughter.

"Sorry," I said. I squeezed my eyes shut as if that would magically make it easier not to laugh. "You rollerbladed?"

"Yes," Robyn said. I opened my eyes again, only to see her sitting on the curb, changing into her rollerblades. "And it's not polite to laugh at people."

"I'm not laughing at you," I said, though it wasn't very convincing since my voice came out very breathy as I tried not to let the laughter out.

"Sure," Robyn said. She put her shoes in her backpack, then picked it up and started to rollerblade away. I quickly jumped on my bike and followed her. I was actually impressed at how fast she could go since I could barely go five feet without falling when I was on rollerblades.

We had to go to a restaurant to get drinks since there wasn't a bar in our town. We sat in a booth in the far corner of the place, beside a large window. When the waitress came, Robyn ordered a glass of wine, and I ordered a beer and a basket of fries. Since we got so little, we had everything on our table five minutes later.

"Willing to share the fries?" Robyn asked with a sly grin.

"Sure," I said. I pushed the basket towards her, and she happily ate one.

It was only then that I realized spending time one-on-one with Robyn meant that I had to keep the conversation going. When we went out as a group, Kiara had always been the most talkative. The silence was deafening, so I broke it the only way I knew how: by talking about the book competition.

"You haven't been reading much," I blurted. I internally face-palmed a second later. I'd meant to ask if she had been reading much, but I knew she hadn't, so the question didn't really make sense.

"No. I haven't." Back to the silence, then. A minute later, she let out a small sigh. "I've just been busy with work and choosing classes for next year."

"You're switching schools, right?"

She looked momentarily shocked, then nodded.

"Kiara tell you?" She asked.

"Yeah," I said. I tapped the tips of my fingers against my beer glass, making a satisfying clinking sound.

"I guess you're not too happy about that," Robyn said. She picked up one of the fries daintily. "Having to go to school with me again."

"I definitely wasn't pleased when I heard the news," I said.

She laughed a little. "Most people wouldn't be honest about that."

"Why lie? We both know it's the truth."

Robyn nodded slowly as she chewed.

"That's what I like about you, Harlee," she said. "You always speak your mind."

Had Robyn just complimented me? No, that was impossible. The closest she'd ever gotten to complimenting me was the stupid back-handed compliments that she loved so much.

"What's the catch?" I asked.

She blinked. "Catch?"

"Yeah. You just said something nice about me. What's the catch?"

She laughed and shook her head. "Like I said, you always speak your mind."

"That doesn't answer my question."

"There's no catch. It was just an observation."

I squinted at her suspiciously, but her words seemed genuine. I wasn't sure how to react to that. Was I supposed to say thank you for noticing? Was I supposed to compliment her back? Was I supposed to just ignore it? I really needed someone to explain the intricacies of talking to your nemesis because the best guide I'd had growing up was Doofenshmirtz and Perry the Platypus, which was not helping me through this situation.

"Oh."

She tilted her head and stared at me. I held her gaze for about ten seconds before I had to break and look at the street beside us.

"Why did you make this reading challenge in the first place?" Robyn asked.

"What do you mean? You're the one who thought you could read more than me. Which you can't, by the way."

"I can and I will," Robyn said reflexively, "but that wasn't what I was talking about. Before that, you already had a goal to read fifty books this summer. What was the motivation behind that?"

I shrugged. "I just wanted to read more. Is that so weird?"

"I guess not," she said. "I just thought there might be more to it."

"I'm afraid not," I said. "I just bought way too many books, and I need to read them fast."

She hummed. "I see."

"Don't do that."

"Do what?"

"Think about me," I said.

"I'm not allowed to think about you, now?"

"You know what I mean."

"I'm not sure I do, honestly."

"Don't try to figure out why I'm doing something or find it interesting."

"I don't recall saying I found it interesting."

"You wouldn't have asked if you weren't interested."

"Well, I thought you were going to say something

interesting, but then you didn't," Robyn shot back. "So no, I don't find it interesting."

"But you would have found it interesting if I had a different answer," I said. "If I'd told you that I made it my mission to read all these books this summer because it was my mom's dying wish."

"Your mom's not dead."

"You don't know that."

"I literally saw her walking down the street yesterday."

"Maybe it was her ghost," I said immediately. Robyn stared at me dubiously, a small smile playing on her lips. "What? We already have vampires in town. Why not ghosts?"

Robyn snorted. "Touché."

I glanced at my watch. It was getting close to ten-thirty, and I did have some stuff I needed to do before I went to sleep. I wasn't working in the morning, at least, but I preferred not to mess up my schedule too much on the weekend.

"I should get going," I said apologetically.

"No worries," Robyn said. She looked at the time as well and whistled. "I didn't realize it was so late, already."

"Time flies when you're..." I hesitated, realizing my mistake too late. I didn't want to suggest that spending time with Robyn was fun, but now I was in too deep not to say it. "Having fun," I finished in a small voice.

Robyn nodded but immediately looked away, digging through her bag for something.

"I'm going to call an Uber home," she said. "It's a

little too far for me to walk, and I can't rollerblade under the influence."

"Of course," I said, trying not to laugh at the reminder that she rollerbladed to work that day. The restaurant was closer to my house than hers, so I didn't mind walking, but I didn't want to leave her there alone. "I'll wait with you."

"Do you want a ride?" She asked.

"No, no, I'm fine to walk," I said. She nodded and finished putting in the request for an Uber. "I'll just go up and pay."

"I can pay for my stuff," she said.

"I don't mind," I said. "It's barely anything. I'll meet you out front?"

She nodded and stood up. I walked inside the restaurant. Unlike most places in the area, customers had to pay at the main counter rather than at the table.

"Hi there, how was everything today?" The woman working asked when I walked up.

"It was great," I said. It only took me a couple of minutes to pay then walk outside to where Robyn was waiting.

"Hey," I said when I walked up beside her. Her screen was open on the Uber app, tracking where her driver was.

"Hey," she said. "She should be here in two minutes."

"Great," I said.

"You know, I just realized I don't have your phone number," Robyn said.

"Oh," I said. She looked at me imploringly. "Yeah, I don't have yours either."

"Do you want it?" She asked slowly.

"Oh! Oh, yeah, that would be great." I really lost all my common sense around her. I pulled my phone out of my pocket and opened the contacts app so she could put her information in. She did so quickly then handed my phone back to me. "I'll just text you, so you have my number too."

I texted her a simple Hey! Her phone dinged a minute later.

"Got it," she said as if there was any confusion. My phone dinged as well a moment later. I assumed it would just be her also saying hi, but when I looked at it, I realized she had actually sent me a gif from one of my favourite movies.

"You like that movie, right?" She asked. "I was pretty sure you did, but we haven't actually talked much, so I wasn't certain."

"Yeah, I love it," I reassured her.

A navy blue car pulled up in front of us. Robyn checked her Uber app to confirm it was the right car.

"This is me," she said, taking an awkward step toward the car door. "Text me when you get home, okay?"

I nodded. "You too."

We had all heard horror stories of people getting kidnapped by their Uber drivers, and while I was sure most of the stories were fake, I would sleep better knowing she was home safe.

She got in the car, and it pulled away. I went to grab my bike. I wasn't really feeling the effects of the drinks, but I wasn't about to bike under the influence, so I began the painful process of walking my bike home.

My phone dinged in my bag when I was a couple of blocks away from my house, and I assumed it was Robyn saying she got home. I didn't want to stop, so I didn't check my phone until I was inside.

Robyn: Home safe.

Robyn: I had a lot of fun tonight. Thanks for inviting me xx

I swallowed thickly, confused by everything that had just happened. Were Robyn and I... friends?

19

ROBYN and I texted sporadically on the weekend, though no significant conversations came of it. I wondered whether she felt strange about this whole thing, too, like she wasn't sure how to feel about this odd and tentative friendship we had formed. When I got to work on Monday morning, she smiled at me. Genuinely smiled. Weirder yet, I found myself smiling back.

"How was your weekend?" She asked.

"Pretty good," I said. "I didn't do much, honestly. How about you?"

"Same," she said. "My sister and I went thrifting on Saturday. That was fun."

"Find anything good?"

She opened her mouth like she was going to say yes, then sighed.

"No," she said resignedly. "It wasn't a great shop."

"Where was it?" Unless one appeared in the last

couple of months without me noticing, our town did not have a thrift shop.

"We went over to West Lemon," she said. "Which I maintain is the most stupid town name I have ever heard."

I laughed. West Lemon was about forty-five minutes away from our town and only marginally bigger. It was known for the lemon festival it had every year, hence the name. The festival was unusual since it was very difficult to grow lemons in our climate.

"I agree," I said. "When I went to university, Kiara and I mentioned the town to our friends, and they thought we were joking."

"The town is a joke," Robyn said.

"It's bigger than East Port, at least."

"But still tiny. And you have to tell people you live in West Lemon every time someone asks you where you're from, so who's the real winner here?" She looked at the clock. "Come on, we need to get out there."

"Do we have to?" I asked, even though I knew the answer.

"Unless you want to lose your job," Robyn said brightly.

"Maybe Tracy won't notice if we're not on the floor," I argued. "Just for a few minutes."

"There are not enough people working here for us to get away with that," Robyn said. When I still didn't move, she grabbed my wrist. Sparks shot up my arm, and I would have ripped it away in shock if she hadn't been pulling me forward. Robyn either didn't feel the sparks, or she was just refusing to acknowledge them, as she just continued walking. "Come on."

Since she was making no big deal out of the situation, I decided it was best that I ignored it as well. I stopped dragging my feet and instead began walking after her. She dropped my arm as we made our way out of the employee area and into the main store.

"I'm on cash this morning," she said. She started walking backwards toward the counter. "I'll see you later, okay?"

I nodded and gave a small wave of goodbye. This was fine. Everything was fine.

About two hours into my shift, the store was more or less empty, and there wasn't much work to be done, so I didn't see any reason for me not to talk to Robyn for a couple minutes. She was fixing a display near the entrance, although I didn't see anything wrong with it. She probably just didn't want to look like she was doing nothing.

"Hey," I said. I lightly bumped my shoulder against hers. It was a bit of an awkward movement since I didn't usually touch people, and I regretted it as soon as I did it.

Luckily, Robyn didn't notice my internal cringing as she smiled at me and said, "Hey." She immediately abandoned her task, offering further proof to my theory that she was just doing it to look busy.

"Do you have plans after work?" I asked. I slipped

my hands in my pockets. "If you're free, we could go to the coffee shop or something."

"Sorry, I'm going out with Celine," Robyn said. "Tomorrow?"

"Sure," I said. I was curious about her going out with Celine since I hadn't heard her mention the other girl since their first date a couple of weeks ago. "How's it going with Celine? I remember you said your first date was great, but you haven't really talked about her since then."

"Oh. Yeah." She tucked her hair behind her ears as she thought. "Honestly, things are kind of fizzling out. That first date went great, but we haven't been texting much since then. I'm going into this date with an open mind, but I think it might be over after this."

"Oh. That's too bad. I'm sorry." She didn't seem all that upset about it, but it just seemed like the right thing to say.

She shrugged. "Better to realize now than later. Oh, I'm going to go help that customer. I'll see you later."

"Bye," I said half-heartedly as she headed to the front of the store, where a customer was looking a little lost.

So, things weren't going as well between Robyn and Celine as I'd initially thought. I smirked, feeling a sense of satisfaction at that idea, then tried to wipe it off my face before Robyn noticed. *You're not supposed to be happy when something goes wrong for your friend.* I was really going to have to change some of my thoughts about Robyn if I wanted this friendship to last at all.

❧ 20 ☙

THE TIME of my lunch break wasn't set in stone, so I ended up eating lunch at wildly different times every day, with different people on the break with me. Most days, I was alone for most of my lunch since we couldn't have many people off the floor. Sometimes, though, I would get those rare days where Robyn and I managed to time our breaks at the exact same time and eat lunch together.

Wednesday was one of those days.

"Hey, do you mind if I ask you about something?" Robyn asked as we finished eating. There was still a little time left in the break, and usually, I would read, but it was nice to be social sometimes, too.

"Sure."

"Why have you been reading so many middle-grade books recently?"

"How do you know which books I've been reading?"

"Goodreads," she said like it was obvious.

"I thought you didn't look at my Goodreads," I said in a teasing tone.

"Shut up."

"No, no, no," I said, waggling my finger in her direction. "You called me a stalker for looking at your Goodreads page, and now you're trying to get away with looking at mine?"

"I'm obviously not getting away with it if I'm talking about it," Robyn said.

"You're trying to act like it's no big deal," I said.

"It isn't a big deal!"

"If you had said that when I was looking at yours, then I would be more inclined to agree with you right now."

"It's not important—"

"Why were you looking at Goodreads anyway? I thought you above that."

"I never said I was above using Goodreads."

"You heavily implied that it wasn't worth your time to look at my page."

"Nothing is not worth my time, at this point. I have all the time in the world."

"Because you're a vampire?"

"Of course," she said dismissively. "Anyway, I saw on your Goodreads that you've been reading almost entirely middle-grade books, and you used to never do that before. What gives?"

I shrugged. "Preferences can change."

"But the whole point of this challenge was to cut down on your physical TBR, and most of those are fantasy books."

I raised my eyebrows. "Wow, you really did a deep dive into my Goodreads page, huh?"

If she knew that, it meant that she had looked through my list of books I wanted to read and compared it to the books I had been reading.

"The days are long when you don't sleep," she said. "And stop changing the subject. It's annoying."

"All the more reason for me to do it, then," I said. "Annoying you is my biggest goal in life."

"You need to dream bigger."

"You need to mind your own business."

She cracked a smile. "Seriously. I thought you were more of a young adult fantasy person. Why middle grade?"

"It's a bit of a long story."

"I've got time." She checked her watch. "In fact, I've got a whole four minutes left in my break."

"Wow. So much time."

She crumpled up a clean napkin and threw it at me. I flinched even though I knew it wouldn't hurt, but it didn't matter anyway because the napkin landed on the floor between us. Robyn stared at it sadly.

"I had such high hopes for that little guy," she said.

"I'm very sorry for your loss."

"Thank you." She sniffled and put a hand to her heart. "He was so young. So full of life."

"He had so much potential," I said. I shook my head. "A life cut short."

Robyn nodded, then looked back up at me.

"Anyway, you were saying?" She prompted in her normal voice.

"I'm not sure I was saying anything," I said. "But I

guess I can explain anyway. It's not a very interesting story, unfortunately. I'm just trying to work my way through the shorter books on my list first, so I finish more books over the summer."

"Don't you miss reading fantasy, though?"

I shrugged. "Sure, but it's not a big deal. I'll go back to it eventually."

"You mean, once you put yourself in a reading slump from reading books that you're not actually enjoying."

"Who says I'm not enjoying them?"

"The look on your face right now," she said flatly. She brushed non-existent crumbs off her legs and stood up. "I'm just saying, it seems like a big waste to restrict what books you're letting yourself read for a challenge. Anyway, I have to get back to work, but I'll see you later."

"See you." I still had five minutes left on my break, and I was planning on using every last one of them, so I stayed where I was.

I thought over Robyn's words. I understood where she was coming from, but I wasn't sure what she was saying really applied to me. Were the books I was reading my favourite in the world? No. But I was planning on reading all of them at some point, so it made sense to do it now, when the number mattered most.

I probably just hadn't explained myself well. Or she was trying to convince me to read longer books since that would take more time and make it harder for her to catch up in the competition again. Yeah, that was probably it. Everything came back to the competition for Robyn and me.

FRIDAY MARKED EXACTLY one week since the day that had changed everything in my and Robyn's rivalry-turned-friendship. Assuming that what we had could be considered a friendship — I wasn't entirely sure what the definition of it was, and honestly, it felt more like a temporary truce than anything.

Part of this truce was biking home together every day. It was really convenient for me since it cut out the awkward ten minutes in which I would wait after my shift ended before leaving work to ensure that I didn't accidentally end up biking beside her on our way home.

"Hey, I saw this cool thing on Instagram the other day," Robyn said as we rode home on Friday afternoon. "It was a 24-hour read-a-thon."

"Read-a-thon?"

"Yeah. You're supposed to read as much as you can in the given time limit, this one being 24 hours."

I did actually know what a read-a-thon was, I was

just surprised at her bringing one up, but I didn't bother to explain that.

"When is it?" I asked.

"Starts tomorrow at 2 p.m. I thought it might be fun for us to participate in it together. It would help us both get ahead in the competition."

"I'm not sure how helpful it is if we both do it," I pointed out. "We'll probably read the same number of books, so we'll still be tied."

Robyn had somehow caught up again in the competition. I was trying not to be petty about it.

"But the competition isn't just about winning," Robyn said. "It's also about reading as many books as possible, right? You said you wanted to cut down on your TBR, and this is the perfect way to do it."

Somewhere along the way, I'd forgotten my real goal for the summer. I'd been so focused on being ahead of Robyn that I hadn't even been looking at how many books I'd managed to read in the summer or if I was on track for that goal.

"Right, of course," I said. While she probably did know how much the competition had distracted me over the summer, I didn't want to mention it. I didn't want her to know how much I cared. "Yeah, that sounds fun. If you want, you can come over while we do it."

"For the whole time?"

I nodded. "I mean, if you don't mind sleeping over, that is."

"Do you think your family would mind if I'm there?"

"Why would they mind?" I asked. I had the house

to myself for the weekend, so I didn't see any reason why they would care, as long as I didn't trash the place.

"Well, they might find it a little weird that I'm staying over," Robyn said slowly. "You know, I'm pretty sure the last time your parents saw me was when I was thirteen."

"Oh, they're not home!" I explained. I was so used to spending time with Kiara, who expected for my family not to be home whenever she came over since that was usually the case, that I forgot that Robyn didn't understand my family's dynamics as much.

"Your whole family isn't going to be home for the whole weekend?" Robyn asked dubiously.

I shook my head. "My parents are going on some romantic getaway or whatever, and my brothers are staying with our grandparents."

"I'm surprised they didn't just leave them with you."

I shrugged. "It's more fun for everyone if the boys are at our grandparents' place. Still free babysitting for my parents, my brothers get to be on a sort of vacation, and I don't have to deal with two screaming children."

Robyn laughed. "Very good point."

We reached the fork in the road where Robyn and I had to split up to go to our respective houses. We both stopped.

"So, do you want to come over for the read-a-thon?" I asked. "I can make us dinner and everything if you want."

"Well, how could I ever turn down an offer like

that?" Robyn asked with a wink. My heart skipped a beat — for a completely unrelated and coincidental reason. "I'll come by around 1:45 if that works for you."

"Sounds great."

Robyn nodded, and we went our separate ways. Now that I wasn't biking next to her, I went a little bit slower. Even though we were on friendly terms, I couldn't let go of my old habits of being better than her at everything, and that included how fast I could ride my bike.

I got home just as my parents were leaving. Based on how quiet the house was, it was safe to say that my brothers were already gone.

"Good day, Harlee?" My mom asked as I walked my bike into the garage. She was standing by the open passenger car door, clearly about to get in.

"Pretty good," I said. I leaned my bike against the wall and hung my helmet on the handlebars.

Mom pinched my cheek, and I grimaced but didn't pull away, not wanting to deal with the argument that would ensue.

"Looks like it was a really good day," she said. "You look happier than you have in a while. Do you have plans for the weekend?"

"I do, actually," I said. "I'm actually spending time with Robyn Huang."

"Robyn?" She asked happily. "That's wonderful! Her mom mentioned to me that Robyn was working at the bookstore this summer, but I completely forgot to tell you that."

It would have been nice to have that warning.

"Yeah, she's been really helping me with learning the ropes at the store," I said. That was embellishing the truth a little bit, but that's what I always did when I talked to my parents about Robyn. They loved her.

"She was always such a nice girl," Mom said fondly. The door from the house to the garage opened, and my dad walked out.

"Ready to hit the road, Julie?" He asked.

"Yes, definitely," Mom said.

"Have a good weekend, Harlee."

"You too."

I slipped inside the house as they got in the car and waved goodbye as the door closed behind me. Once they were gone, I laid down on the couch and sighed.

Robyn Huang is coming over to my house tomorrow. What is my life?

❧

As I expected, I won the bet, and Robyn was a sore loser about the whole thing.

"You only won because you're reading those short books," she muttered. She dug into the pizza we ordered for lunch.

"A book's a book," I said in a sing-song voice.

"Keep telling yourself that."

"Hey, middle-grade books are valid reading material."

"I don't disagree," she said. "I'm just saying that maybe we should have based our various bets on page count rather than the number of books. To make it more fair, you know?"

"That is a very good point," I conceded. "It's too bad you didn't bring it up when we were first creating the rules for the challenge."

"You added a rule partway in!" Robyn shot back. "The rule about updating Goodreads once a day."

"That was about sharing information during the challenge — which we should have been doing anyway, might I add. You're suggesting changing how the challenge itself works because you're mad that you're losing."

"We're actually tied right now," Robyn said. "You may have won this battle, but you're going to lose the war."

I shrugged, trying to look as disinterested and unfazed as possible. "We'll see."

"All this is beside the point, anyway!" Robyn said suddenly. I looked at her with an amused grin.

"What is the point, exactly, then?" I asked.

"Who decided that you are the almighty ruler of this competition?" Robyn asked. She raised an eyebrow. "Hm?"

"I'm not the almighty ruler," I said. "We're doing what I say because I am able to back it up with valid reasoning, rather than just my emotions. And if I was the almighty ruler, it would be because this whole thing was my challenge in the first place — this bet is just piggybacking on my plan to read fifty books this summer."

"Yeah, well..." She cut herself off. "Okay, I don't

have a response to that right now. But know that I am still mad about this."

"It's duly noted," I said dryly.

"And don't patronize me."

"I can't do both."

Robyn glared at me. I smiled back cheekily and blew her a kiss. Out of character for me, sure, but that was what she did to me. And if she ever told someone about it, then I would just have to kill her.

❧   2 2   ☙

Dear Kiara,

I sighed and dropped my pencil again. I'd promised to write to Kiara at least twice a week but even just three weeks after she left, I was running out of things to tell her about. I decided I would start it the same way I started all my letters, and Kiara would just have to deal with it if she wanted me to continue writing her letters so frequently because there was only so much I could say. Her argument had been that I was used to writing since I was an English Major, and I'd responded that I was fantastic at writing essays, not letters. If she wanted me to send her weekly essays analyzing a classic book, I would have no trouble doing so.

How are you? I hope you're having a lot of fun at camp!

. . .

I tried to remember what she'd written in her last letter so I could play off of that a little, but I couldn't remember for the life of me. I knew exactly where the letter was — laying on the upper left corner of my desk, with the paper neatly placed back in the yellow envelope it had come in — but I was in the kitchen and way too lazy to go upstairs to get it. I remembered her saying something about an old camp friend and some scheme to get people to start dating for some reason, but without specifics, I couldn't bring any of that up.

Or are you secretly wishing you were here with me instead? Oh, who am I kidding? You're obviously having more fun there than you would be here. I wouldn't be surprised if you ended up living there full-time to run the year-round activities.

That was the best I could do talking about her, so now I had to shift the focus of the letter to me. In theory, that was easy enough, but in practice, it was actually rather tricky. I had very little going on in my life. I gave her an update on the reading challenge in every letter, although I doubted she cared all that much, and told her any of the limited town gossip, but that was all.

In my last couple of letters, though, there had been one topic I was avoiding talking about at all costs: Robyn. It wasn't that I was trying to keep secrets from Kiara or anything. I just knew that if I said I became friends with Robyn within two weeks of Kiara being gone, then Kiara would get all 'I told you she was so sweet' and 'oh my gosh, I can't believe I managed to get you two to like each other,' and I really didn't want to have to deal with that.

Robyn and I had been talking and spending time with each other for a week and a half by that point, though, so I had to bring it up soon. I was pretty sure Robyn was writing to Kiara too, though not as frequently as me, and she was bound to bring it up at some point. If she mentioned it before me, then I would never hear the end of it from Kiara. She would go on about how she thought we were best friends but couldn't possibly be if I was keeping such an important piece of information about her, and while it wasn't too serious, she would keep it going forever. She still brought up the fact that I didn't tell her about my first girlfriend until a week after our first date. That was from seven years ago.

So, it would have to be in this letter.

I'm not sure if you talk to Robyn I erased that instantly. Thank goodness I was writing this in pencil. I knew for certain that the two of them spoke to each other, and I was sure it was pretty frequently.

In case Robyn didn't tell you No, I couldn't say that either because it made it sound like I was only telling her because Robyn didn't, and she would get just as annoyed about that.

I have something I've been meaning to tell you That was much too dramatic and made it obvious that I had been harbouring this secret for a while.

I needed to make it more casual. Instead of starting the paragraph by telling her about Robyn, I had to lead into it with something about the competition. That way, bringing up Robyn was just natural.

Clearly, Kiara constantly bringing up that old story really made me re-evaluate how and when I told her news.

Since you left, I've gotten a lot of reading done, just like expected. I'm almost at 50 books for the summer, and there are still three weeks left! Robyn's been reading a lot too. We've actually started hanging out sometimes to read and talk about the competition. Of course, we talk about some other stuff too, but mainly it's about the competition.

Can't wait for you to come home! I know you always want the summer to last forever, but I'm ready to move back to school.

I know there are four more weeks of camp left, but when are you coming home for a visit again?

Love you!
Harlee

. . .

Perfect. Well, maybe not perfect, but it was the best I was going to do. I quickly folded the paper and slipped it into the prepared envelope I had in front of me. I had ten minutes to get the letter into the postal box at the end of my street if I wanted it to be collected that evening. I tried to send my letters out on the same day every week, so Kiara knew when to expect one from me.

I had to run a little to get there in time, but I managed to get it in the mailbox just as the delivery truck was pulling up. Thank goodness for the small victories in life.

❧ 23 ☙

On Thursday night, my family and I had a rare dinner with all of us there. Usually, even on the days when we were all home, my brothers had to eat early, before whatever extra-curricular they had. They were both supposed to have baseball practice that day, but it was thunder storming, so it was cancelled.

"So, Harlee," Mom said, halfway through the meal, "you and Robyn are getting pretty close now, aren't you?"

"I guess," I said hesitantly. I was a little worried to see where she was going with this. Historically, any time my mom brought up Robyn out of the blue, it meant she was planning something.

"I was thinking, we haven't seen her in so long," Mom said.

I groaned. "We're not going out for dinner with her family."

"I wasn't going to suggest that," Mom said.

"You weren't?" I asked, raising my eyebrow.

"No. I was actually going to say that we should invite Robyn over for dinner one day."

The thought of that was at least a little more palatable. Robyn's parents were nice enough, but I didn't have anything in common with either of them, and only our moms got along. Our dads would usually sit there in silence since they also didn't have much in common. And, of course, Robyn and I hated each other, so we would usually end up seeing who could kick the other the hardest under the table without our parents noticing or do some stupid challenges, like who could name more words that started with the letter X.

"We can never even manage to have dinner as a family," I said. "You really want to add a sixth person into that equation?"

Mom gestured around the table.

"We're having dinner as a family tonight," she said.

"Yeah, for like the first time in a month!"

"Well, the boys don't need to be there," she said. "They don't even know Robyn anyway. It can be just the four of us."

"I don't think that solves the problem."

"We'll do it next Tuesday," Mom said, completely ignoring my comment.

"Why Tuesday?" I asked with a frown.

"It's the only evening your father and I are both free."

"Okay," I sighed. I didn't really want this to happen, but I wasn't against it enough to argue with my mother over it. She was fantastic at debating, so I rarely won when I tried to go against her.

"Of course, you'll need to ask her if she's free," Mom said. She looked pointedly at my phone, which was lying face down beside my plate.

"I'll do it tonight," I said. Robyn and I rarely texted, and we never called, but this was a situation where I preferred to call her. I hoped that I might be able to way her into saying no, even if she was free.

"Why not do it now?" Mom asked. "While you're thinking of it."

"Because you instilled in me that it's rude to use my phone at the table," I shot back. "I'll call her later. Leave it alone."

"You're going to forget."

"I'm not going to forget," I said, rolling my eyes.

"Yes, you will," Mom said. "You're going to forget, and by the time you remember, it will be too late, and she'll have made other plans."

I rarely forgot to do anything, so her argument was baseless, but I knew she would continue to harp on me.

"Why do you care about this so much? You haven't seen her in five years. I'm sure you can wait another couple of weeks."

"Isn't the fact that it's been five years reason enough?" Mom asked rhetorically. "Just text her."

I sighed loudly but did as she asked. I wasn't willing to outright tell Robyn to say no over text since that left evidence that my mom might find out about, but I did my best to convey the thought all the same.

. . .

Harlee: Hey, my mom wants to know if you want to come over for dinner next Tuesday night. Totally fine if you're not free, though!

"There. I sent it." I put my phone down again.

"Was that so hard?"

My mom went back to eating while I tried not to clench my hand into a fist. While I probably wasn't the best role model for my brothers, I did my best to not seem like a terrible person in front of them. I just didn't understand why my mom was so concerned about Robyn coming over for dinner.

My phone pinged a couple of minutes later.

Robyn: Our moms are definitely planning something because my mom is insisting that I come.

Well, that cleared up the mystery a little bit more. They were probably so excited that Robyn and I were friends that they wanted us to spend all the time in the world together. Never mind that every dinner our families had together usually ended with Robyn and I screaming at each other, and our moms insisting that their child is the worse one — which, of course, was fantastic for our self-esteem. In fact, the last time we all went out, Robyn ended up punching me just before we got in the car. Of course, our parents didn't see, and Robyn claimed I had just fallen and hurt myself.

. . .

Harlee: Yay.

"She said she's free," I said resignedly. I knew that the dinner probably wouldn't be as bad as I was anticipating, but that didn't stop the knot of dread that had landed in my stomach.

Robyn: Cheer up. I promise I won't punch you this time.

I snorted. At least one thing would be different with this dinner; being friends with Robyn might actually make it bearable.

ℜ 24 ℜ

"I'm just saying, I don't understand why guys in books always have those weird scars," Robyn said emphatically. We were sitting at the coffee shop near the bookstore after work on Monday afternoon. "I mean, does anyone in the world have genuinely interesting scars?"

"Kiara has a cool birthmark," I said. It only registered to me a moment later that a birthmark was probably not considered in the same league as a scar.

"What constitutes a cool birthmark?" Robyn asked.

"It's on her back, and it's shaped like Florida," I said. "So, I guess that's the only criteria in my mind."

Robyn stared at me blankly for a few seconds, just long enough for me to regret saying anything at all. Then she laughed, and relief washed through me.

"Okay, fair enough," she said. "But still, scars. Like, do you have any cool scars?"

"Do I look like someone with cool scars?" I asked blandly.

She shrugged. "You remind me a little of the main character from a fantasy book, so maybe."

"Is that supposed to be a compliment? Because it doesn't sound like one."

"More of an observation than anything."

"Hm." I wasn't offended by the comment, but I was sure how to react to it either. I decided to brush it aside. I stuck out my left leg beside the table so she could see it and pointed at the small pink scar on my knee. "I have the standard scar on my knee that every single person on this planet has."

Robyn laughed. "It's a common scar, but the story is unique to you. How did you get it?"

I had been looking at my leg, but my head snapped up at the question.

"You don't remember?" I asked.

"Should I?"

"I would say so."

"Was I there?"

I rolled my eyes. "No, Robyn, I expect you to remember an event that you didn't witness. Of course, you were there!"

"Okay, okay, I was just asking! No need to bite my head off."

I just huffed.

"When was it exactly?" Robyn asked. "Maybe I can narrow it down."

"Elementary school."

"Can you get any more specific?"

"Grade five. We were on school grounds."

"Okay, that helps." She tapped her finger against her lip. "Was it that time you fell off the playground?"

I stared at her. "Which time? I fell off that playground like once a week.:

"You know…" Robyn said. "The time."

"You're just trying to see if I'll give you the answer," I said.

"No, I'm not!" She said. I glared at her. "Okay, maybe I am. But it's only because I feel bad that you remember this incident so vividly, and I don't."

"You don't have to feel bad," I muttered.

"But I do," Robyn said. "So, will you please tell me the story?"

I thought about it for a moment. "No."

"Harlee, tell me," Robyn whined. I shook my head. "Come on, it obviously has something to do with me."

"Hell yes, it has something to do with you," I said. I crossed my arms and leaned back. "Which is why I find it so rude that you don't even remember!"

"I promise I will never forget it again if you tell me!" Robyn said. She drew a little cross over her heart.

"You can't make a promise like that," I said.

"But I am," Robyn said. She looked at me with wide, innocent eyes. "For you."

"Stop looking at me like that. It's weird."

"I'll stop if you tell me the story."

I wanted to say no, but she kept staring at me with those big eyes, and I broke within ten seconds.

"Okay, fine." I sat up a little straighter like I was going to make an important speech, rather than just tell her some stupid story about us from nine years ago. "It was in the spring of our fifth-grade year."

"As you previously established."

"I said it was grade five, not that it was spring. Now hush, I'm setting the stage." I cleared my throat. "It was the spring of our fifth-grade year. You, me, Jessa, and Katie all had new bikes, and we decided we wanted to see who could go the fastest. Naturally, the place to do this was the hill behind the school since it was grass and would hurt less if we fell."

"Which also meant it was way bumpier," Robyn added.

"Yeah, it was not a well-thought-out plan," I agreed. "Anyway, we were going down that hill. I think Jessa was in the lead, and you were in second. I was at the end of the row, and you were beside me. I was starting to catch up to you, and I guess you didn't want me to come even close to winning because you swerved suddenly. Obviously, I had to swerve to avoid you, and I fell off the bike and hurt my knee."

"Oh..." Robyn said. "I have no recollection of this."

"Well, it happened. And the scar on my knee isn't the only one, now that I think of it. I also have one on my wrist." I held up my wrist, so she could see the small scar on it. After a moment's hesitation, I added snidely, "You never said sorry, either."

I didn't want her to think that I still cared about some stupid incident that happened nine years ago or was waiting for an apology. If anything, my comment was more about the fact that Robyn had never apologized for anything she had done to me, this being one of many times that she had wronged me in my life.

Robyn pulled my wrist toward her. Before I could

understand what she was doing, she gently pressed her lips to my scar, like she was kissing it better. Then she looked me in the eyes and whispered, "I'm sorry."

Despite it being about one small, practically insignificant day from years before, that apology meant the world to me.

❦   25   ❦

W HEN ROBYN CAME over for dinner the next night, I made sure I was the one who opened the door. We'd spoken briefly on our way home from work about the dinner, but I wanted to try to talk to her before my mom started her interrogation.

"Hey!" Robyn said. She was wearing the same burgundy dress that she'd worn a few weeks prior, when we'd gone out for dinner with Kiara. In fact, she looked almost exactly the same as she had that day, down to the curled hair and the chic silver necklace hanging from her neck. She was also holding a small gift-wrapped box in her hands. "I'm not late, am I?"

"It's hard to be late when you're the only guest."

I stepped aside so she could come in.

"Well, there was an agreed-upon time for me to be here," Robyn said, "so coming later than that would generally constitute as late."

"You're not late," I said with a slight eye roll.

"Okay, I just wanted to make sure." She glanced down the hall. "Are your parents in the kitchen?"

"Yes." I grabbed her elbow and pulled her back gently when she tried to walk in that direction. "But I wanted to talk to you before we went in there."

Her eyebrows knit together. "Why? Is everything okay?" She looked over her outfit. "Do I have something on my dress?"

"You look fine," I reassured. "I just thought we should have a bit of a... game plan in place for this dinner."

"A game plan?" Robyn asked, an amused grin on her lips.

"Yes," I said. "There's the obvious: avoid talking about politics and religion."

"Harlee, believe it or not, I have had dinner with your parents before."

"And it has never ended well," I shot back.

Robyn put her hand over mine, gently prying it off her elbow.

"It will be fine," she said. "I promise."

I would have argued, but my mom chose that moment to walk down the hallway.

"Harlee, haven't you invited our guest in yet?" She asked.

"She's in the house," I muttered.

"Robyn, it's so lovely to see you," Mom said, completely ignoring me.

"It's nice to see you too, Mrs.Dunn," Robyn said kindly. She held out the box in her hands. "For you."

"Oh, you shouldn't have," Mom said.

"I'll be in the kitchen," I said, brushing past them.

I wasn't in the mood to deal with the small talk that was going to endure for the next ten minutes.

Dad was in the kitchen, putting the finishing touches on dinner. On the rare occasions we didn't order food, my parents liked to cook together. I never understood why. If anyone even stood within a ten-foot radius of me while I was cooking, I was ready to kill them.

"Do you need any help?" I asked. I only asked to be polite — I knew he was going to say no. There had never been a time in my life when my parents had taken me up on my offer to help with dinner.

"No thanks, honey," Dad said. "I'm almost finished, anyway."

"Okay." With nothing better to do, I sat down at the table. Robyn and Mom walked into the room a minute later, and Robyn took the seat across from me while Mom went to help with dinner.

"Thanks for leaving me alone with your mom," Robyn murmured. The kitchen and dining room were really just one open space, so she had to say it incredibly quietly for my mom not to hear.

"Having me there would not have helped the situation," I murmured back in the same tone.

We didn't say anything else until dinner was on the table, and everyone had served themselves food.

"So, Robyn," Mom said as she settled in, "your mom tells me you're transferring universities."

"I am," Robyn said. She made eye contact with me, and we were both thinking the same thing: this dinner was starting to make a lot more sense.

"What program are you in, again?" Mom asked.

"I'm in business," Robyn said.

"That sounds like a good degree," Mom said. "Very useful. Unlike something in, say, the humanities."

My hand tightened around my glass of water, and I bit my lip. Now was neither the time nor place for me to explain to my parents, yet again, why I was in studying English Literature.

Robyn's eyes darted between me, Mom, and Dad, who was eating peacefully and ignoring the conversation at hand.

"All degrees have their uses," she said diplomatically.

"Some more than others," Mom said.

"Why don't we talk about something else?" I interjected. "Robyn, how's your family?"

Robyn went on a long spiel about her family, and Mom nodded along politely even though we all knew she spoke to Mrs.Huang as much as I spoke to Robyn. After that, the conversations stayed in a pretty safe zone throughout dinner, with my parents asking Robyn all about her plans for the future (since there's nothing else to talk to university students about, of course) but not making any jabs at me for the most part. But, of course, my mom had to ruin it during dessert.

"Robyn, you were in the gifted program in high school, right?" Mom asked.

Robyn took a sip of the coffee Mom had just placed in front of her.

"I was," she confirmed. Mom smiled and shook her head fondly.

"You always were so smart," she said. "And valedictorian too!"

I choked on my drink, drawing all eyes to me.

"Sorry. Swallowed wrong." I cleared my throat. "I didn't realize you were valedictorian in high school."

"Of course, you know Harlee was valedictorian at your eighth-grade graduation," Mom said, "but that doesn't hold a light to high school."

Gee, thanks, Mom. This was what our moms always did — they both loved to insist that their own daughter wasn't the better one of the pair for some reason. The issue here was that Robyn's mom wasn't here to balance out all the negative things my mom was saying about me.

"They're both great achievements," Robyn said with a tight smile.

"Two achievements can be great, but that doesn't mean one isn't greater than the other," Mom said.

"Right," Robyn said. I narrowed my eyes; she couldn't even try to argue something in my defence?

Mom started asking Robyn about her grades and scholarships, which seemed like incredibly invasive questions to me, but Robyn answered all of them happily. At first, I was surprised at her willingness to share everything with my mom, but after a few minutes, I realized I wasn't actually surprised at all. Robyn thrived on adults telling her how great she was. I started to zone out a little bit, just like I used to do when I would go out with Robyn and Kiara. I was forced to sit there and half-listen to their conversation for another half-an-hour before it finally began to come to a close.

"Do you want more coffee, dear?" Mom asked Robyn.

"Oh, no, thank you," Robyn said. "I really should head out now, before it gets too dark."

"Of course," Mom said.

"Walk me home?" Robyn asked me. I gave a jerky nod, although I wanted to say no. We both got up and walked out. Neither of us said anything as we left, except to mention when to turn, considering there were many paths to her house.

"Let's cut through the field," Robyn said. "It's faster."

"Okay."

Our old elementary school was in the middle of town, surrounded by fields on all sides. The playground was in the dead centre of it, and though we'd found it fun when we were kids, I was a little creeped out by it now. In the dark, the large expanse of land looked exactly like the kind of place a serial killer would hide.

When we got to the playground itself, Robyn went to sit on one of the swings. I stood a couple feet away.

"Listen," Robyn said. "I'm sorry that I was talking about myself so much at dinner. I know you didn't invite me over, so I could just go on and on about myself. Your mom just kept asking me questions and—"

"You didn't seem to mind it," I muttered. I kicked the sand underfoot gently. "I thought you loved getting to brag about how great you are."

"Excuse me?" Robyn asked.

"What? You're the perfect Robyn Huang, unable

to do anything wrong." My tone was dripping with sarcasm. She narrowed her eyes at me then stood abruptly.

"I think I can walk the rest of the way home myself," she said.

"Good," I said. "I don't want to see you anyway."

It looked like our streak of bad endings to family dinners was holding strong.

26

I WAS USED to arguing with Robyn, but I wasn't used to wanting to make up with her afterward. She and I barely said two words to each other for the next three days, and anything we did say was entirely related to work. It was evident that I needed to talk to her, but I knew work was not the place to do that. Not that I could have if I wanted to — Robyn avoided me like the plague whenever we were there.

I only managed to catch up with her on Friday, just as we were leaving work. She was unlocking her bike, but she froze when I stood next to her. Still, she didn't say anything.

"Hey," I said.

She slowly stood and stared at me.

"Hey," she replied. "You need something?"

I took a deep breath and looked just over her shoulder, unable to get the words out when I was looking her in the eyes.

"I'm sorry about what I said the other day. I didn't mean to suggest that I didn't want to talk to you."

Of course, there were other things said that day, but I thought the apology encompassed the worst of it.

Robyn crossed her arms over her chest. "You didn't just suggest it. You stated it outright."

I nodded and swallowed thickly. "I know. I'm sorry."

Robyn stared at me for another moment. "It's fine. Is that all?"

I was taken aback by her brisk words. She really couldn't wait to get away from me.

"Well, I was going to ask if you wanted to do something this afternoon," I said, "but I guess you would say no."

"I'm surprised you would even ask me," Robyn said. She tilted her head. "Who would want to spend time with someone who loves to brag about how great they are, right?"

"I get it," I said tightly.

"No, I don't think you do," Robyn said, her voice rising with each word. "What the hell did you want me to do? Just sit there and pretend that I didn't have any accomplishments so I could boost your ego?"

"This isn't about my ego."

"What is it about, then?" Robyn spread her hands. "What else could it be about? You just can't deal with the fact that I'm more successful than you!"

"I beg your pardon?" I asked. I hoped that I heard her wrong.

She crossed her arms. "You've always been jealous of me."

"I am not jealous of you!" I said. "What planet are you on?"

"Don't even try to hide it, Harlee! The only reason you got so mad about what I said was because you thought you were finally better than me, and you realized you were wrong."

"God, I should have known that you haven't changed," I said. I shook my head and took a couple of steps back. "You're just the same girl that wanted to tear me down every time I did better at something."

"I tore you down?" Robyn asked incredulously. She put a hand to her chest. "I haven't been able to do a single thing this summer without you there to remind me how much better you are than me!"

"That was just the competition—"

"Except it wasn't, was it?" She yelled. Her voice cracked a bit. "You were just waiting for me to mess up! You were just waiting for a reason to hate me again!"

"No, I wasn't!"

"Yes, you were! The second that I said something you didn't like, you decided we couldn't be friends anymore. That was on you!" She poked her finger against my chest, hard enough that it hurt a little.

That wasn't what I'd meant to say or even imply when we were arguing, so the accusation made my blood boil.

"Really?" I asked. "Because right now, it feels like you're the one making that decision."

I spun on my heel and went back inside. If I

stayed there any longer, one of us was going to say something we'd regret, something we couldn't take back.

⚜

Kiara only came home for one night in the whole summer, so it worked out well for me that it was the one weekend I needed her the most. She got home on Saturday evening, just hours after my second argument with Robyn, and we were supposed to go out for dinner, but she nixed that plan as soon as she arrived at my house.

"What happened?" She asked.

"I don't know what you're talking about," I said. I grabbed my purse. "Let's go."

I tried to step out of the house, but she pushed me back inside and followed me in.

"You're upset," she said, crossing her arms. "What's going on?"

I'd been planning to talk it through with her the following day, so I could at least give her one fun evening off from work before burdening her with my issues, but that clearly wasn't happening.

I rubbed a hand over my face. "I had an argument with Robyn. It was nothing."

She raised her eyebrows. "You're this upset over an argument with Robyn Huang? You love arguing with her."

"Not anymore."

Her eyebrows knit together. I didn't see why she was so confused; I had been updating her in my letters for the past couple of weeks. She knew Robyn and I were friends.

"You two are closer than I thought," she said. She walked into the living room and sat on the couch.

"What are you doing?" I asked.

"Sitting?"

"We're going out."

"It can wait."

I sighed and walked over to sit with her. Before I knew it, I was telling her about everything that had happened while she was gone, starting with Robyn and me going out for drinks all the way up until the day before. If there's one thing to say about Kiara, she's a good listener. She didn't interrupt me at all as I went through the whole thing, except to ask some clarifying questions.

"I don't understand why you got so angry about the other," Kiara said. "I know you find it annoying when she brags, but it wasn't like she was doing it just to annoy you. Your mom was asking her questions."

"She should have changed the subject," I muttered. Even as I said it, I recognized the issue in my words. I was putting all the blame on Robyn, when it wasn't her fault at all.

"You're not mad at her," Kiara said. "You're mad at your mom for what she said. Which is nothing new."

That was an understatement. There hadn't been a time since before I was a teenager that my mom and I didn't have a tumultuous relationship.

"She was acting just like she used to," I said. "I thought she changed."

"I'm going to have to disagree with you there,"

Kiara said. "I don't think she's acting like she used to at all."

"Are you kidding?" I asked. "Bragging about all her accomplishments, going on and on about how great she is? That is exactly how she used to act."

"Harlee, it's not like she just waltzed into your house and started talking about herself," Kiara laughed. "And besides, you said it yourself; she tried to apologize for talking about herself when you guys were walking home. You just didn't give her the chance to say anything."

I didn't want to add that part to the story, but the argument only started because of it, so I couldn't really get around it.

"I'm sure it wasn't a genuine apology."

Kiara sighed. "I'm going to be honest with you, Harlee; I agree with Robyn here."

I glared at her. "You're supposed to be on my side. That's what best friends do."

"Some, maybe," Kiara said. "But wouldn't you rather I help you see where she's coming from instead of blindly siding with you?"

"No," I muttered.

"Well, I'm going to do it anyway," Kiara said cheerfully. In a normal tone, she said, "You may have thought that you forgave Robyn for everything she's done in the past, but you haven't."

"Yes, I have!" I said. I waved my arm around. "I— I've been hanging out with her and having a good time. I'm friends with her! Or, I was before all this."

Kiara shook her head and looked at me sympathetically. "If you had, then this wouldn't have bothered you so much. And generally, if you're really friends with someone, an argument over something this minor wouldn't ruin everything."

"I tried to talk to her!" I defended. "I tried to fix it, and she yelled at me."

"I'm not saying she didn't have a part to play in all of this," Kiara quickly clarified. "But it never should have even gotten to that point. You were so sure that she hadn't changed that the second she acted the way she used to, you jumped down her throat."

I sighed, finally seeing what she was saying. Robyn was completely right in what she had said — I'd been looking for a reason to get mad at her, even if I hadn't realized it myself. I thought I had let go of my past hatred, but it was very clear that I hadn't.

"But what can I do about it now?" I asked. I hugged my knees to my chest and rested my chin upon them. "She won't want to talk to me. Not after this."

"You'd be amazed how far an apology can go," Kiara said softly. She stood up. "But, it's up to you what you do. Why don't we get dinner now, and you can think it over this weekend?"

"Yeah," I said. I stood as well. "Okay."

I already felt bad about taking up this much of her time when she got such little time off, so I resolved not to mention it for the rest of the night.

27

I PLANNED to talk to Robyn on Monday, but I couldn't find her anywhere. I knew she was working that day, so I wasn't really sure how it was possible, but she managed to elude me for the whole shift. I would see her from across the store and walk over, but by the time I got there, she would be gone. It was like a game of cat and mouse.

On Tuesday, she managed to avoid me for most of the shift again, but we ended up in the employee lounge at the same time at the end of the day. I tried to start a conversation, but she ducked out of the room so quickly that I almost started talking to the wall. I followed her out, but she was speed-walking out of the store.

She had been leaving like that every day since our fight, and I could only assume she was doing it to avoid me, but I really needed to talk to her, so I ran after her. I reached her before she even got to the bike rack, which meant that she wouldn't be able to take off before I said my piece.

"Hey," I said, falling in step beside her. She kept staring straight ahead.

"I don't want to talk to you right now, Harlee," she said.

"Do you really want to spend the next four weeks like this?" I asked. "More than that, actually, since you're switching to my university, too."

"It's a big place," she said. "We won't even have to see each other."

"You being friends with my roommate might put a wrench in that plan," I pointed out.

She stopped and looked at me with an exasperated expression.

"Fine," she said, crossing her arms. "What's up?"

"I'm sorry," I said. "About everything. I shouldn't have gotten mad at you after the dinner, and I shouldn't have blown up at you last week."

Robyn took a deep breath and closed her eyes. For a second, I thought she was getting ready to scream at me. But when she opened her eyes again, she dropped her arms and looked apologetic.

"No, last week wasn't your fault," she said. "I shouldn't have freaked out at you like that when you were trying to apologize."

I shook my head. "Seriously, it's fine. You were right. I was looking for a reason to get mad at you."

She grinned slightly. "You know, I find it interesting that I understand you so well. Probably more than most of my friends."

"Keep your friends close and your enemies closer," I said.

She snorted. "True."

I sighed. "So, what do you say we go out for coffee?" I smiled teasingly. "Like old times?"

Robyn laughed slightly. "Ah yes, the good old days. As fun as that sounds, I actually have plans tonight. Thursday?"

"Thursday it is," I said with a nod. "What are you up to tonight? Going out with Celine again?"

"Hm? Oh, no, I haven't seen her in a few weeks." She shrugged. "As predicted, it just fizzled out."

"And you thought she was so perfect."

"I know," she said, dragging out the word. She shook her head. "I think part of the problem was that she was so perfect, you know? I can't be with someone who likes me that much."

"Can't say somebody liking me too much has ever been a reason for one of my break-ups, but hey, what do I know?"

She rolled her eyes. "Thanks, that makes me feel so much better."

I punched her shoulder lightly. "Better luck next time."

She looked over me appraisingly. "Yeah. Next time."

I felt like the wind had been knocked out of me. Robyn continued to stare at me intently, and I was suddenly uncomfortable with the energy between us, so I cleared my throat and gestured at my bike.

"I should, uh, get going now," I said in a strangled voice.

"Yeah," she said. "Me too."

She wasn't going home, so we didn't bike together, but I still felt like her eyes were on me the whole way home.

❧ 28 ❧

Despite our conversation, Robyn and I didn't talk very much over the next couple of days. Work had suddenly gotten very busy, so we couldn't talk there, and for some reason, we left at different times on both Wednesday and Thursday, so we didn't bike home together. On Friday, our breaks overlapped by a couple of minutes, so Robyn caught me as she was walking into the break room and I was walking out.

"Hey," she said. "What time do you finish today?"

"Uh... three."

She sighed. "I was going to ask if you want to bike home together, but I finish at four."

For reasons unclear to me, my heart warmed at the mere idea of Robyn wanting to bike home with me.

"We could get coffee or something?" I suggested. "I'll just wait for you at the cafe."

"You don't mind?" She asked.

I shook my head. "As long as I've got a book, I'm happy to wait for hours."

She grinned. "Perfect. I'll meet you there."

I got back to work with a little spring in my step.

Robyn had fantastic timing because she walked into the cafe that afternoon just as I finished the last page of my book. I waved her over to my table.

"Hey, how are you?" I asked when she sat down. It was such a simple question, and it should have been fine. It would have been, except that Robyn asked the same thing at the same time, and because my brain simply does not work, I responded with, "Thanks!"

Robyn blinked. "What?"

"You said how are you, so I said good, thanks," I said slowly.

"But you didn't say good," she said.

I frowned. "What? Of course, I did."

"No." She tried to hold back her laughter but failed miserably. "No, I said how are you and said thanks. That did not answer the question."

"You didn't answer the question either!" I shot back.

"At least I didn't say thanks!"

"Whatever." My cheeks were turning red, so I stood up. "I need a refill."

I went to stand in line, thankful that Robyn didn't follow me. It usually took a lot to embarrass me, but it seemed like any time I floundered even slightly in front of Robyn, I couldn't look at her. I guess I just wanted to impress her more than the average person.

I chose not to question why because I had a feeling I would not like the answer.

When I got back to the table, drink in hand, Robyn was reading the back of my book — my trashy romance book that was verging on erotica — with a smirk on her face. I quickly put my cup down and tried to pull the book out of her hand, but she held on tight.

"I didn't know you liked this kind of thing," she said. She pulled back hard enough that I lost my grip on the book.

"Give it back," I said. I tried to grab it again, but she held it out in the opposite direction, shaking her head. She clicked her tongue.

"I mean, I understand the appeal," she said. "But Harlee, really? 'Fiercely romantic, deeply sexy...'. And oh my gosh, it's a vampire romance too! How did I miss that?"

I finally managed to snatch the book out of her hand. I stuffed it in my bag as she continued to cackle.

"It's a good book," I muttered.

"I don't doubt it," Robyn said, but the laughter still escaping her lips didn't help her case.

"Shut up," I said. I kicked her under the table. "It's not like you've never read anything like this before."

"I haven't, actually," she said. She wiped at her eyes as if she was laughing so hard that she'd begun to cry. I was sure it was all for show. "Am I missing out?"

"Yes."

She nodded. "Okay. I'll keep it in mind."

The ensuing silence was extremely uncomfortable

for me. I finally broke it by asking, "So, are you going to go up and order?"

"Oh," Robyn said. She looked around like she was only just realizing we were in a coffee shop. She stood. "Right. Yes."

She went up to order but came back less than a minute later, her hands empty.

"Changed your mind?" I asked.

"I ordered the drink, just thought I'd wait over here."

"Why?"

"I don't know," she said with a shrug. "But I guess I can wait over there if you'd rather. Let you get back to your... what did that review call it? 'Thrilling vampire saga'."

I tried to throw a napkin at her, but the plan failed before it could really get started. When I tried to pull the napkin off the table, I didn't realize her phone was sitting on top of it, so it went clattering to the floor.

Robyn gasped loudly and crouched down to get it.

"I'm so sorry!" I said. "Did I break it?"

She turned it over in her hands. Luckily, she had a strong case on it, so everything looked fine besides a minor scratch on her screen protector.

She looked at me. "I want a refund on our friendship," she said flatly. Usually, I probably would have been offended by someone saying something like that, but I knew that was just Robyn's sense of humour, so I snorted. "Jokes on you, I'm not even worth a dollar."

Robyn slid back into her chair and looked at me intently.

"You're worth a hell of a lot more than that, Harlee."

My heart leapt into my throat.

"Careful, Robyn," I said. I tried to sound casual, but my voice came out strained, even to my own ears. "If you keep saying stuff like that, then people might start to think that you like me."

She grinned. "Well, we can't have that, now can we?"

I shook my head. "Definitely not."

She continued to stare at me, and I stared back, unable to pull away. Her eyes were beautiful, a deep brown colour. Had they always sparkled like that, or had something changed recently?

"Large coffee for Robyn!" The barista called out. Robyn looked away, and our little bubble popped. What the fuck had I been doing thinking about Robyn's eyes?

"Hey, I was just thinking," Robyn said as she sat back down. I shook my head, trying to clear it of any of my previous thoughts and focused on Robyn. "It's the fifteenth this weekend, which means it's the end of the reading challenge. We're still on for that, right?"

I smiled. "Hell yeah."

She held out her hand for a fist bump, and I obliged. At least everything felt somewhat normal again.

❧ 29 ❦

THE DOORBELL at my house was loud and obnoxious. I was just finishing reading my book when it went off on Sunday evening, two weeks before Kiara came home from camp.

"Harlee, can you get that?" My mom called. "It's probably the pizza delivery person. The money's on the front table!"

I hopped off my barstool at the island and ran down the hallway, then swung the door open, ready to thank the delivery person. The words died on my lips when I saw who was standing on the doorstep.

"Hey," Robyn said. She shifted from foot to foot, looking more unsure than I'd ever seen her. "I hope you don't mind that I came by unannounced."

"I don't mind at all," I said. I glanced behind me, where my parents and brothers were setting the table. I didn't want to bring Robyn into the house, so I stepped out on the porch with her, gently closing the door behind me. "What's up?"

"The competition ends today," she said. She scratched the back of her head with one hand, her other full with a small bag. "We didn't set a time that it officially ends but given that you're more than five books ahead, I don't think there's any way I'll be able to beat you in the day."

"I don't know," I said. "Weirder things have happened."

She grinned. "Love the vote of confidence, but I think this race is over. So... congratulations."

"Thank you," I said genuinely.

She held the bag out to me. "Sorry, it's not gift-wrapped or anything. I'm not sure where my parents keep the gift bags, and I'm terrible at wrapping, so this was the best I could do."

"You didn't have to get me anything." Remembering the original rules of the bet, I added, "Except, you know, my ten bucks."

She smiled again. She was so pretty when she smiled. Who was I kidding? She was beautiful all the time, in a way that made my heart skip a beat.

"Don't worry, it's in there too," she said. "But I thought you deserved a little something more."

"What is it?" I asked dubiously. When we were kids, Robyn had been pretty into pranks and gag gifts, and I was a little worried to see what might pop out of the bag.

"It's nothing bad," Robyn reassured me. "It's a genuine gift."

I was still a little concerned, but I reached in regardless. My hand hit something solid, and I pulled it out into the light.

I gasped. "Is this..."

"Book fifteen of the Secret Tales series," Robyn said. "Open it."

I opened it to the first page, and a small envelope fell down. I just managed to catch it before it fell to the floor. I put the book back in the bag so I could open the envelope more easily. There was a card that said CONGRATULATIONS with a drawing of a dog underneath, which was utterly adorable. Inside, Robyn had written Congrats on winning again. I'm sorry I ruined your original book, but I hope this makes up for it. Underneath was a ten-dollar bill taped to the card.

"What do you mean 'again'?" I asked.

"Well, you know," she said. A light blush graced her cheeks. "You got valedictorian, and I ruined your book as revenge because I couldn't handle the fact that you won. I'm sorry about that."

"It's okay," I whispered. Warmth spread through my chest. "Believe it or not, I'm not angry about it anymore."

I meant it. There was no way I could still be angry when she had just given me such a lovely and thoughtful gift.

"Well, I'm glad about that, or this next thing would be really awkward."

I frowned in confusion. "Next thing?"

"Yeah." She cleared her throat. "I was wondering... if you might want to go on a date with me sometime?"

She sounded so unsure as she asked, like she really thought I was going to say no, but she wanted to ask anyway, just in case. My heart melted a little.

"Yes," I whispered. In a slightly louder voice, I said, "Yes, I would love to go on a date with you."

Relief spread across her face. "Really?"

I nodded. "Really."

She glanced at my closed front door, then back at me. "Would it be all right... if I kissed you?"

I understood her hesitance. My family was right inside, and at any moment, one of them could walk out, trying to figure out where the pizza was or why I'd been outside for so long. But this moment was too perfect, these emotions too raw, to pass up, so I closed the small space between us and pressed my lips against hers.

I guess you're not my sworn enemy anymore.

❧ 30 ❧

"I'm sorry," Robyn said as we walked out of the movie theatre the next Friday night. Since Robyn had asked me out, she chose the date, and she went with the classic dinner and a movie.

I slipped my hand into hers as we walked out in the chilly evening air.

"About what?" I asked.

"I really thought that movie would be a lot better than it was," she said. "I mean, it looked so good in the trailers."

"I liked it."

Surprise crossed her face, then doubt a moment later.

"Really?" She asked suspiciously.

I shrugged. "Yeah. I'm not a very harsh movie critic."

"Unlike with books."

I frowned. "I'm not a harsh book critic, either."

"You once again forget that I follow you on Goodreads. You tear those books to shreds."

"I do not!"

"Just yesterday, you gave a book one star and said you wished you could get back the hours you wasted on reading it."

I paused. "That was a one-time thing. I'm normally very nice in my reviews."

"Mh-hm."

She spun around, so she was standing in front of me instead of walking beside me. I barely managed to stop myself from walking straight into her.

"Hey," she said. "Can I ask you something?"

"Of course," I said. I tilted my head. "You gonna propose?"

She laughed. "No, I'll only do that after the second date."

"Oh right, we have to move in together after the first date," I said. "Silly me."

We were still holding hands, but she reached out to grab my other one as well. Her silver rings were cold against my skin, causing goosebumps to run up my arm. It all felt so intimate.

"You were going to ask something," I reminded her when she didn't say anything for a minute.

She grinned cheekily. "Will you be my girlfriend?"

I stared at her for a moment, my brain taking its time to catch up with the situation. Robyn Huang was asking me to be her girlfriend. Me.

"Of course," I whispered.

Finally, we were both winning together.

CHECK OUT BOOK ONE OF THE SAPPHIC
SUMEMR SERIES, *SCARLET SUN*.

I always thought the summer after my first year of university would be magical. After all, I was returning home after eight months of living in residence — I would get to spend time with my family again, I could eat actually good food instead of the junk they served in the cafeteria, I wouldn't have to share a bathroom with thirty other girls, and, most of all, I would have my own room.

I definitely over-idealized that idea in my mind.

My family was annoying me to no end, I apparently remembered my parents' cooking wrong because it tasted barely better than what I had in the cafeteria at school, sharing a bathroom with my little sister was somehow worse than sharing it with thirty other college girls, and though having my own room was nice, it was also a total mess (and I would never admit this, but I missed my roommate, Elyssa).

I kicked my now empty duffel bag across the room and ran my hands through my hair. I had finally finished unpacking after coming home, but although my clothes were nearly put away, the rest of my room was still in disarray.

"I thought I was supposed to be relaxing after exams," I muttered to myself as I turned to clean up my desk. I'd meant to clean my room before leaving for school so I wouldn't have to deal with it when I came back, but of course, my laziness had won out, and I'd left the problem for my future self. Now cursing my past self for making that decision, I began the tedious task of sorting through the massive piles of paper on my desk. I pulled my small recycling bin over to beside the desk and began throwing out everything that I no longer needed.

There was a small knock on the door.

"Come in!" I called. I turned to see who was there. In the doorway was my eight-year-old sister, Jean. I smiled. Although we had a twelve-year age difference, I always enjoyed spending time with my sister. "Hey Jeanie. What's up?"

"What are you doing?" Jean asked, walking into the room.

"I'm decluttering my room. Want to help?"

Jean shrugged. "Sure."

"Can you sort through the papers and tell me if any of them don't look like they came from a school notebook?" I asked, pointing to a stack of papers on the main part of the desk. Most of them were old high school notes, but I worried about throwing them out without at least confirming that there wasn't anything important in the pile.

"Okay!" Jean said, bouncing on her toes.

"Thank you," I said, ruffling her hair briefly.

I went back to sorting through my own pile, but it was only thirty seconds later that I was interrupted by Jean going, "Hey what's this?"

I looked over as Jean tugged a small paper out of the middle of the pile, almost toppling the whole thing over. She held the page triumphantly. Unlike the other standard notebook pages, it was light pink and had drawings of flowers at the top.

"It looks like it's from my old diary," I muttered. I gently took the paper out of Jean's hands and looked it over. At the top of the page, it said, 20 THINGS I WANT TO DO BEFORE I'M 20. Underneath was a list:

1. Go skinny dipping
2. Get a tattoo
3. Go on a road trip
4. Go camping in Algonquin
5. Watch the sunrise
6. Hike a mountain
7. Learn how to drive
8. Dance in the rain
9. Conquer a fear
10. Swim in the ocean
11. Fall in love — real love
12. Dye my hair
13. Read 100 books in one year
14. Learn a second language
15. Run a 10K
16. Learn how to play an instrument
17. Graduate high school
18. Donate blood
19. Be out and proud
20. Make a new list: 30 things to do before 30

Jean looked at me with wide, curious eyes.

"Well?" She prompted when I didn't say anything.

She put her fists on her hips and tapped her foot. "What is it?"

"It's nothing," I said. I put the paper on the top shelf of my desk, much higher than she could reach, and turned back to the task at hand. "Just some stupid list I wrote in high school."

Jean crossed her arms and looked up at the paper that was out of her reach with a large sigh. I rolled my eyes. She really needed to learn that she was not entitled to everything just because she wanted it.

"Are you going to help me, or just stand there pouting?" I asked. Jean sighed quite loudly again, but then grabbed another small pile of papers to sort through. We worked in silence for a couple of minutes before Jean couldn't hold in her questions anymore.

"What kind of list was it?" She asked.

I shrugged, not looking up from the papers in my hands. "Just a list."

"Right, but what kind of list?"

Recognizing that Jean would not give up until she got what she considered a satisfactory answer, I said, "It's a list of things I wanted to do by this summer."

Jean frowned. "Why this summer?"

"Because I turn twenty years old this summer," I said. I threw a stack of old high school tests in the recycling bin beside me. "There were some things I wanted to do before my twentieth birthday."

Jean nodded solemnly. "How many have you completed?"

"I don't know," I said.

"All of them?"

"Definitely not."

"But some of them?"

"Yeah, I think so."

Jean huffed, getting tired of my short answers. "Are you going to finish them?"

"I don't know," I said.

Jean huffed again. "I'm going downstairs."

"Okay."

Jean faltered, as though she expected I to stop her. I assumed she was only pretending to want to leave in the hopes that I would ask her to stay. Then, she would use wanting to know more about the list as leverage. But I could see straight through her.

"I'm really leaving," Jean said. She took a step closer to the door. I glanced up.

"Okay, I'll see you later."

Jean frowned, but she did walk out. I shut the door behind her, then tried to get back to work. But within a couple of minutes, I found myself distracted again. What was on that list? I hadn't looked it over very carefully before. How many of the items had I completed? Which ones were left? Was it possible for me to finish it before my birthday in two months?

I grabbed the list from the shelf and looked it over. Skinny dipping? I had never done that. Get a tattoo? I already had two. I glanced over the rest of the list. I wagered that I'd done about half of the items on the list. Whether or not I wanted to do the rest was a toss-up. Some of them were easy: dance in the rain, watch the sunrise, dye my hair. But some of them would be much harder, whether it be from an organizational standpoint or an emotional one: go on a road trip, conquer a fear, fall in love. I supposed if I really dedicated some time to it, I might be able to finish them, but it would definitely take a lot of effort.

I grabbed my phone and sent a picture of the list to my best friends group chat with the text, *think I can manage it?* It was a resounding yes from Bree and Kiara, ever the optimists, while Elyssa seemed unsure, and Harlee said there was absolutely no way. Although I knew Harlee was probably joking, hearing someone tell me I couldn't do it made me want to try even more.

If there was one thing I enjoyed in life, it was proving people wrong.

CHAPTER 2

On Friday afternoon, I drove the two hours from my house to Kiara's house in another town. Part of the fun, if you could call it that, of making friends at university was that we all lived in different towns. Of everyone I met, none were from the same town as me — although I was admittedly from a pretty small place, so that was not unexpected. But none of my friends were even from the same town as each other, save for Kiara and Harlee who had been best friends for years and had chosen to go to university together. My friends lived all over the province, all over the country in fact, and that made it incredibly inconvenient to visit them.

I tapped my hands against the steering wheel to the beat of the music as I drove along. Whenever my favourite songs came on, which were few and far between, mind you, I sang along to them. I enjoyed singing along to music when I drove, but I hated the idea of somebody seeing me. While for the most part, I tried to ignore what other thought of me, I could never shake the feeling of how stupid I must look when I was doing so.

It was the first time I was ever visiting Kiara's house. I had visited the town, East Port, only once before, for Harlee's New Year's Eve party. I hadn't had time nor reason to go to Kiara's house on that day. As such, I had no idea that Kiara's house was quite so far. My GPS led me down a long winding road that, if I hadn't had a map right in front of me telling me otherwise, I would have said leads straight out of town. Even though I was certain I'd put the address in right and I trusted that Kiara had given me the right address, I kept checking the GPS every minute or two, as if it was going to suddenly change and tell me I was going the wrong way. The longer I drove down this empty road, the more uneasy I felt. My grip on the steering wheel was so tight that the skin over my knuckles had gone completely white. When a squirrel ran in front of my car, I nearly screamed. I slammed on the brakes so hard that my body slammed forward, the seat belt digging into my neck. I had to take a couple of moments to collect myself.

Maybe I shouldn't have watched that horror movie last night.

I'm not usually a fan of horror movies, but Elyssa kept raving about it to me and I had to see what the fuss was about. Personally, I don't think it was all that good, but I didn't tell her that.

I also didn't tell her that I screamed more than once while watching it. I have a reputation to maintain, after all.

I glanced at my GPS again. It said I was finally approaching my destination, but when I looked ahead, all I saw was open road. I frowned and turned down my music, as if that would help me find my way at all. I heard my dad's voice in my head: *I can't see when you play your music that loud! Turn it down.* I never understood him saying that until I learned to drive myself and had the same issue.

Finally, the GPS told me to turn right at the next road. It appeared out of nowhere, but once I turned on it, I breathed a sigh of relief as I saw a line of houses. For some reason, this seemed to be a small suburban neighbourhood that was greatly disconnected from the rest of the town. Kiara's house was only one block in. I turned into the driveway and parked in front of the closed garage doors, just like she told me to. By the time I climbed out of the car, Kiara and Harlee were walking out the front door.

"April!" Kiara called. She ran down the front steps, and more or less tackled me in a hug, knocking the breath out of me. If you've ever gotten hugged by a girl who played hockey in high school, you'll understand the feeling. She pulled back again, though she kept her hands planted firmly on my upper arms, and smiled widely. "How are you? I've missed you so much!"

"I'm good, Kiara," I said. "I've missed you too. But it has only been two weeks."

"Two weeks is way too long!" Kiara said. She glanced back at Harlee, who was standing a few feet behind her, with an amused look on her face. "Isn't it Harlee?"

Harlee nodded ever-so-slightly. I think, like me, she thought that two weeks was hardly anything, but she didn't want to disagree with Kiara.

"We're happy you could visit so soon," she said.

To my surprise, I found that they both looked a

bit different than they had when I'd seen them last. Harlee was beautiful as ever; her long and dark brown hair was shiny and sleek, her makeup was perfectly done (her eyeliner was sharp enough to cut somebody with — I'd never understood how she did it), and she had clearly just gotten a manicure, as she had light pink acrylics on her hands. It was a far cry from how she'd looked throughout exam season, where she'd barely bothered to get ready every morning before she started to study.

Kiara, on the other hand, had made a much more drastic change.

"You cut your hair!" I exclaimed. I ran my fingers through the ends of her strawberry blonde hair, which now just reached her chin in a chic bob. For as long as I'd known her, and I believe for most of her life actually, Kiara had kept her hair long. Like, extremely long. By the time she had started university, it was well past her waist.

"I did," she said. She ran a hand through it, shifting it from a right part to a left one. "Do you like it?"

"It looks awesome!" I said. "It really suits you."

She beamed. "Thank you!"

"Do you need help carrying your stuff in?" Harlee asked. She held a hand up to block the sun from her eyes.

"It's fine, I don't have a lot." I popped open my trunk and grabbed the small duffel bag I'd brought for the trip. My keys and phone were already in my hands, so I had everything I might need for the weekend. "Actually, can one of you close the trunk for me?"

"Yeah, I've got it," Kiara said.

"Thanks." I frowned and looked around. At first, I had assumed that Bree was busy doing something in the house and that was why she hadn't come to greet me outside, but I didn't see her car anywhere around. "Is Bree not here yet?"

"No, she hit traffic on the way here," Kiara said. The trunk slammed closed. "She should arrive soon though."

"Okay," I said.

Unfortunately, Elyssa wasn't able to come for just the weekend since she lived so far away from us.

"Come on, I'll show you around," Kiara said. She grabbed my hand and pulled me forward. The house was big and very open concept. As soon as we stepped inside, I could see most of the main floor, except for the section that was blocked by the stairs. The house was pretty modern, with dark hardwood floors, leather furniture, and sleek black appliances. Although there were sheer blinds covering all the windows, the house was full of natural light. "My bedroom is upstairs, but we were thinking of sleeping in the basement instead since it's a lot bigger. Are you okay with that?"

Honestly, I was a little wary of going down to the basement after watching that horror movie but I didn't want to mess up her plans, so I said, "Yeah, that's fine."

"Great!" Kiara said. She continued to pull me forward. "So obviously this is the main floor. As you can see, the dining room is here, the kitchen is up ahead, and the living room is across from it. The sliding glass doors over there lead out to the backyard, but there's also a door from the basement that we'll probably use more often."

She opened the door to the basement and turned on the light. As we walked down the white stairs, I was relieved to see that the basement was also very open concept and bright, unlike the one in the horror movie. We walked to the far end, where there were three couches forming a semi-circle around a TV that was mounted on the wall above the fireplace.

"This is where we're going to sleep," Kiara explained. "We can either sleep on the couches, or we can use the air mattresses. We just have to get them out of the garage and set them up."

"And hope that they actually work this time," Harlee said with a small grin. "I seem to remember the last time we used those air mattresses, they deflated every twenty minutes."

"Only one of them did!" Kiara defended. "But you're right, the couches would probably be better. We've also got some futon cushions that we can put on the floor."

"All this is to say, we have options," Harlee said. She clapped her hands together. "Can we go to the hot tub now?"

Kiara rolled her eyes. "Sorry about her, she's been asking to go to the hot tub since she got here."

"The fact that you have a hot tub is the only reason I have remained friends with you for so long." She said it in a serious voice, but when I glanced over at her, I could see the humour in her eyes.

"And just for that, you don't get to use the hot tub," Kiara said.

"Hey!"

"Is there somewhere I can get changed?" I asked. I gestured uselessly at my clothes. "I'm not really dressed for going swimming."

"Oh yeah, of course!" Kiara said. She pointed at a bathroom down the hall. "You can get changed in there if you want."

"Thanks." I grabbed a swimsuit and beach dress from my bag and went down the hall. Although Kiara, Harlee and Elyssa were all more than comfortable changing in front of each other, I generally preferred some privacy.

In the bathroom, I quickly got changed, then pulled my light brown hair out of the ponytail I had been wearing it in while I was driving. I smoothed down my locks as best I could, although it still looked like a mess. I sighed and stared at myself in the mirror. Whatever, I was about to go swimming — what did it matter what my hair looked like? Leaving it as it was, I walked back down the hall.

Kiara and Harlee were standing by the door and each scrolling on their phone, but they perked up when I walked back. I dumped my driving clothes back in my bag, grabbed my sunglasses, and slipped on my flip-flops.

"Let's go," I said.

The large pool took up a good portion of the back-yard. Beside it were a line of lawn chairs, set up perfectly in the sun. Closer to the house, and under the shade of the overhang, was the hot tub. Kiara and Harlee immediately headed there, but I hung back.

"You okay?" Kiara asked when she noticed.

"Yeah, I think I would just rather tan for a bit," I said.

"Here, I'll move one of the chairs closer to the hot tub for you," she said. Kiara was much physically stronger than me, so I stood by patiently as she picked up one of the chairs with ease and moved it closer, while still leaving it in the sun. "Is that good?"

"It's great," I said. "Thanks."

I kicked off my shoes and sat down. I was just settling in when I heard the telltale sound of Bree's truck. Well, it was really her older sister's truck but Bree used it more than her, so it was like it was hers. I groaned as I stood up again. We walked around the side of the house to meet her in the driveway.

"Hey guys!" Bree said, waving at us wildly. Just as she did with me, Kiara ran up to hug her, while Harlee and I hung back for the time being. Bree hugged Kiara back just as enthusiastically, then began fawning over her new haircut.

"My haircut?" Kiara said. "What about yours? It looks fantastic!"

"I didn't get a haircut," Bree laughed. Kiara rolled her eyes.

"I meant your extensions, Bree," she said, shoving her shoulders. With them standing next to each other like that, it looked like they had switched hairstyles. Where Kiara had gone from long hair to a bob, Bree had gone from shoulder-length hair to mid-back length hair. It was dirty blonde and naturally straight, though she had curled it that day. She'd begun growing out her hair in the middle of high school, when she officially came out as trans, but it was a long process to grow it out from how short it had been before, and I knew she had always wanted really long hair.

"It does look very good, Bree," I said. "When did you get it done?"

"Just a couple of days ago," she said with a grin. "It was a present from my parents. So what are we doing today?"

"Well, we were thinking of just sitting in the hot tub for a little while," Kiara said, gesturing to the fact that we were all in beach wear, "then this afternoon, maybe going into town. I know Harlee wanted to go to the bookstore this weekend."

"I just got my final pay check from my job at school and now I want to go spend it," Harlee said. We all laughed, full well knowing that we did the same whenever we got our pay checks.

"That sounds like fun," Bree said. "I just need to change into my swimsuit."

"Oh yeah, no problem," Kiara said. "I'll show you around inside. Harlee and April, you guys can go back to the yard. We'll meet you there in a minute."

"Okay," Harlee said.

When we got back there, Harlee immediately slipped into the hot tub, but I took up my seat in the sun again.

"It's warmer than I expected," I said. I wasn't sure why I said it exactly. I had always thought that making small talk was worse than just not talking at all, and it wasn't like Harlee and I didn't have any other things to talk about. The words just slipped out before I had time to think it over or stop them, and it would be weird if I tried to take them back.

"A bit strange for May," Harlee agreed. She shrugged. "But you never know what the weather will be like around here."

I hummed in agreement, then wracked my brain for anything else to say. I hadn't spoken to anyone outside my family since getting home from university, and it had apparently had an effect on my social skills.

"So what books are you planning to buy when we go into town?" I asked.

"I'm not sure yet. I've got a pretty long list of books I want, but honestly, half the time when I go into a bookstore, I buy a ton of books that I've never even heard of."

"Thereby making your list even longer."

"Exactly." She grabbed a pack of gum from her bag and popped a piece in her mouth. She held up the packet so I could see it. "Want one?"

"Sure." I moved from my seat by the pool to be sitting next to the hot tub, though I didn't climb it. I still found the afternoon air too warm to warrant getting in the hot tub. I wasn't sure how Harlee was managing it. "What flavour is it?"

She flipped the packet over so she could read the name.

"Extreme mint," she read out. "Whatever that means."

It did seem rather ambiguous, but I just shrugged. The patio door opened, and Kiara and Bree walked out, now both dressed in bathing suits. Kiara also had some towels under her arm. It was a good forethought that hadn't even occurred to me.

"Either of you want gum?" Harlee asked. Kiara shook her head, but Bree held out her hand. Harlee popped out a piece for her, before putting the pack back in her bag.

Bree came and sat next to me, then bumped her shoulder against mine.

"Hey, we didn't really get to talk earlier," she said. "How's it going?"

I just shrugged in response. When she continued to stare at me, I cracked and said, "I'm okay."

"You like being home again?" She asked curiously. To be honest, I didn't hate it as much as I thought I would, but it still wasn't my favourite experience. I knew the answer she was looking for, so I just snorted and shook my head. She nodded and squinted up at the sky. Her long hair fell back. "Yeah, me neither."

"I thought you liked spending time with your family."

"I do. But I miss being with you guys more than I like being with them."

Normally Bree didn't say stuff like that. Harlee was the one who spoke in a way that made you stop and think. It made sense, given that she was studying English Literature. So when Bree said that, I had to take a moment to consider it.

"I wouldn't have expected you to compare the experiences," I said finally. Because that was also what Bree was like. She had an optimistic view of the world, and never liked to compare the present to the past, or long for what once was.

She grinned slightly, but still didn't look at me. "I guess you guys are slowly changing me."

"The best friends do," Harlee said with a wink. I laughed hollowly along with them, but there was a small ache in my heart at Bree's words. I didn't want to change her. I wasn't trying to change her. Bree was perfect just as she was, and I would never want to do anything to compromise that.

The conversation turned, but I didn't follow it after that point. I grabbed my phone and opened up my messages. I had a couple of texts from people that I glanced at but didn't bother responding to. I would get to them later. I was pretty sure that most of my family and friends had learned to expect my responses to any non-urgent texts to come in at midnight or later, since I liked to catch up on my messages before I went to bed.

"Isn't that right, April?" Kiara asked. I looked up in surprise. All three of them were looking at me.

"Sorry, I wasn't listening," I said, slipping my phone back into my bag.

"It's fine. I was just complaining about our history professor from last semester," Kiara said.

"Enough talk about school!" Bree said. "I don't want to think about that until September."

"What do you want to talk about, then?" Kiara asked.

Bree shrugged. "Your house is awesome. How long do you have it to yourself?"

"Just the weekend," Kiara said. "My parents will be back Monday evening. Oh, by the way, does anyone want a Palm Bay? I have a bunch in the fridge."

"You want to day drink?" Bree asked with an amused smile.

"Hey, we're on vacation!" Kiara defended. She hopped out of the water. "I'm assuming you all want one. I'll be right back."

Harlee and Bree laughed as she walked away.

"I love summer break," Bree said.

WITCHES
IN LOVE
ISABEL HANSEN

Mira always knew she was going to lose her powers when she was sixteen, but that didn't make it any easier when the day actually came around. Her mother always told her she shouldn't just assume that she would lose her powers after the Becoming Ceremony, but as the certifiable worst witch in the coven, Mira thought even entertaining the possibility that she might pass was absurd.

The Becoming Ceremony only ran twice a year, on the solstices, and it had to be done in the year a witch turned sixteen, so Mira only had two chances. She had already royally failed the first time around, so pretty much any confidence she'd had earlier in her life had long since gone out the window.

So there she was on the Winter Solstice, attempting to get ready. The dress she had to wear was way too long for her; it was more of a gown than anything. Between it being white and the way it trailed behind her, Mira felt more like she was getting married than going through her Becoming Ceremony.

Mira walked over to the mirror hanging on the wall. Surprisingly, there was nobody standing there, all of them seemingly too busy whispering with their friends about what the test may entail to care about their appearance. The only design on the dress was a small rune stitched directly on the centre of the chest in emerald green thread. Mira knew the rune well, having seen it many times in her life; in her coven, the High Priestess bestowed a rune upon every child when they go through the First Rite. Mira's was the symbol for *undying love*.

Mira saw Emma approach in the mirror but didn't register it until she bumped her shoulder against hers. Rather than looking at her best friend directly, Mira made eye contact with her in the mirror.

"How are you feeling?" Emma asked. Mira wondered if she could see the nervousness on Mira's face or the way her hand was shaking slightly as it brushed the rune on her chest. She was trying to hide how scared she was, but most people could probably see through her. She was the worst witch in the coven, after all — if anyone was going to fail today, it would be her.

"Good!" Mira said as brightly as she could. Emma looked at her dubiously. Mira tried to force her smile to be more genuine, though that was pretty much impossible. *Think of something happy. Puppies! Puppies are great. Why isn't this working?* Mira couldn't even trick herself into thinking it looked genuine since she was staring at herself in the mirror.

"Yeah?"

"Yeah, I'm great," Mira said. She nodded her head to make her point but didn't stop, so she ended up turning into a bobblehead. Lying through her teeth, she said, "This is going to go so well."

Emma frowned. "You don't need to lie to me, Mira. I can see that you're nervous."

"I'm not nervous." She hoped if she said it enough times, it would become true. So far, it wasn't working.

"Right. Of course not," Emma said. She turned, so she wasn't looking at Mira anymore, though their shoulders were still lightly touching. "Did you see the Queen of Darkness over there?"

Mira turned to look at where Emma was gesturing. It wasn't hard to spot. In the far corner of the room, Lola Johnson was standing by herself with a glower on her face. She looked strange in the white gown, the clothes contrasting her dark makeup. Mira thought it was the first time she'd ever seen her in non-dark clothing.

"LJ?" Mira asked, as if there was anyone else Emma might refer to as the 'Queen of Darkness'. "What about her?"

"Some of the other girls are taking bets on what skill she'll try to show off in the magical component," Emma said.

The first part of the Becoming Ceremony was often referred to as the magical component. It was pretty much a test to ensure that you could do magic even somewhat competently. When Mira had attempted the test six months earlier, on the Summer Solstice, the priestess testing her had taken pity and told her that she could just leave after Mira set off fireworks while attempting a water spell. Technically, the priestesses weren't allowed to tell them if they had passed until the whole Ceremony was over and the witches weren't supposed to leave early, but Mira thought it was best for everyone that she didn't continue. She could only pray that she would do better this time; it was her last chance.

"Oh?" Mira said when Emma didn't continue.

"Yeah. Sarah thinks she's going to try necromancy."

Her stomach dropped at just the mention of the word.

"Necromancy?" Mira asked in a small voice. "But... but that's illegal!"

There was no way LJ would try that, would she? Not in the Becoming Ceremony, at least. Although LJ seemed to believe that rules were optional, Mira didn't think even she was stupid enough to do something blatantly illegal in front of a priestess.

Emma smirked and crossed her arms, her eyes trained on LJ.

"You think she cares about that? I bet she finds it fun."

Mira bit her lip and looked at LJ again. Was Emma right? Mira could only imagine the chaos that would ensue if a witch got arrested in the middle of a Ceremony. It wouldn't bode well for her, that's for sure. Or maybe it could work in her favour — Mira could convince the priestess running her exam that Mira only struggled on the magical component because of everything going on. That was believable, right?

Mira was so lost in her thoughts that Emma had to nudge her multiple times to get her attention. Mira looked at her, wanting to ask why, but a hush had fallen over the room. Emma subtly jerked her head in the direction of the doorway, where the High Priestess was entering. On instinct, Mira stood up a little straighter and watched her.

The High Priestess paced at the end of the hallway

for a moment, then stopped abruptly and spun on her heel to face the girls.

"Good evening, everyone," she said. She spoke softly, but her voice echoed through the room. "And welcome to this year's Becoming Ceremony."

This solstice's Becoming Ceremony, Mira thought. *But it's nice of her to pretend that we didn't all fail last time.*

It wasn't a fair thought, she reasoned. There were definitely many people in her year who simply chose not to try the Ceremony back in June, knowing that they wouldn't pass and not wanting to shake their confidence in their abilities. They weren't all like her.

The High Priestess looked over the collection of teenagers. She only made eye contact with Mira for a moment, the briefest of moments, but it felt like an eternity to Mira as a shiver went up her spine. She always felt like the High Priestess could see into her soul whenever she looked at her.

"If you're all ready," the High Priestess continued, her voice crisp, "please follow me."

She spun on her heel again, her black cloak flowing around her and the silver rune on the back shimmering in the light. She was the only person in the coven who wore her cloak on a daily basis, since they were only required at all the official ceremonies. It was technically suggested that the cloaks be worn Every day, but the tradition had slowly faded away over the years.

The group of sixteen-year-olds followed her out of the room in a single-file line. The mansion the coven worked in was large, but Mira had the hallways memorized. The hallways she knew about, that is. Witches-in-training were only allowed in a small part of the coven mansion, and Mira had no idea what secrets may lay deeper in the building.

The hallways the High Priestess led them through were a labyrinth. Mira tried to keep track, mainly as a way to focus on something other than her nerves, but she lost track after they went up two flights of stairs then seemingly turned back around the way they came. She wondered if the High Priestess was taking them to their destination by an unusual path to confuse them — though, the only reason Mira could think of for doing that was in case the High Priestess was worried any of them were going to fail and would try to break into the mansion at a later date. All witches who passed the Becoming Ceremony could go where they wanted through the building, after all, so there was no reason to hide the actual path now.

They went down so many staircases that Mira was certain they must have been in the basement, but when the High Priestess finally slowed down, they were standing in an atrium at ground level. They were facing a large wall of windows and a glass door that led to a beautiful garden, filled with a hedge maze. There was a sign on the hedge that Mira squinted to see, but once she did, she was sure she must have misread it; she could have sworn that it read DANGEROUS. ENTER AT YOUR OWN PERIL.

Emma's chin rested on Mira's shoulder, which was an awkward position to walk in. Mira consciously slowed her steps and tried to avoid raising her shoulders in a way that would hit Emma's chin hard.

"I hope we're going outside," Emma whispered.

Her breath tickled Mira's ear, and she worked hard not to cringe.

"I doubt it," Mira whispered back. Up ahead, the line was stopping.

"Do you think we'll be allowed in the garden after we pass?"

There was another twinge of doubt in Mira's heart at Emma's word. She didn't know if she could pass. She didn't think she was going to, but she couldn't say that.

"I hope so," she whispered back, electing not to mention the sign. It was probably a joke. The garden looked too beautiful to be dangerous, and she felt a tugging sensation in her stomach, pulling her towards it. She glanced at the window again. *It's probably not that amazing anyway.*

They moved from a line into a semi-circle surrounding the High Priestess. The witches all moved in synchronization, used to this after years in the coven.

"You will be called by the priestesses one at a time to do the magical component of the Becoming Ceremony," the High Priestess said. She looked at the group seriously. "This is to test your magical abilities. You will not be informed after the test whether you have passed or failed."

She made eye contact with Mira as she said this. Mira took a deep breath and blinked back the tears that were threatening to spill over her eyes. Nobody was looking in her direction, but she felt like everyone was staring at her, judging her, and thinking about how she was the one who was going to fail.

The High Priestess continued looking around and Mira breathed a sigh of relief, though she was no less stressed.

"You may leave at any time, but by doing so, you are guaranteeing failure." The tone it was said in made it clear that it wasn't really an option. "I highly recommend you do not do so. I wish to see you all on the other side."

One of the doors to the left of the High Priestess opened. Mira heard it but could not drag her eyes over there. Five priestesses created a line along the wall with the window. Their air was strict and foreboding; Mira felt like she was going to suffocate. She was going to suffocate in an open room.

One of the priestesses stepped forward.

"Mira Carson."

Mira's stomach dropped, even as Emma squeezed her hand and whispered, "Good luck."

Here goes nothing.

LJ STANDS UP FOR HERSELF FOR ONCE IN HER MISERABLE LIFE

Lola Johnson sometimes wished she was never born as a witch. She wished she could have just been a normal kid, like all those oblivious humans at school. Having magic was great, of course, but if she'd been born as a human, then she never would have known what she was missing anyway.

And she never would have ended up kneeling here in a long white gown, somewhat scared for her life.

From the angle she was at, all LJ could see was Priestess Reed pacing back and forth in front of an altar. The click of her boots hitting the wood floors echoed across the walls, each one making LJ flinch.

Is this what the Becoming Ceremony is supposed to be, or is she just trying to make me squirm? The thought had crossed her mind three times since she got in there. Everything just seemed off to her, and it wouldn't surprise her if it was purposeful — the two of them had never seen eye-to-eye after all.

Her heart was in her throat. LJ was not usually one to be scared, but she wasn't entirely sure she wasn't about to be killed. Executed. As the priestess continued to pace, LJ wondered how the coven would go about executions. Burning at the stake seemed like the obvious choice, given its rich history, but it didn't seem like their style. Perhaps beheading. She was already kneeling, so all they would need to do would make her lean just a little bit forward, get an axe (or maybe they would go with a guillotine) above her, and then BAM — before she knew it, she would be missing her head.

LJ had to stop herself from looking up to check that there was no executioner there.

The sharp sound of Priestess Reed's feet snapping together as she came to a stop broke LJ out of her musings. She wasn't about to be executed. She was in the Becoming Ceremony.

"You have a good future ahead of you, Miss Johnson," Priestess Reed said in a quiet tone. Quiet yet commanding. LJ shivered. "Dare I say, you are the best witch this coven has seen in more than three centuries."

"Thank you, Priestess," LJ whispered. She didn't pretend to be surprised by the compliment. While she had perhaps not known that she was the best in quite that much time, it was obvious to her that she had a talent few in the coven possessed.

"Still, you are not perfect... not by any means. And so I must remind you of the gravity of the promises you are making today."

LJ's heart pounded a little harder, the sound filling her ears. She remained silent as the priestess took a step closer to her.

"Do you swear your life to the coven, Miss Johnson?"

LJ's head immediately snapped up. She stared at the priestess with wide eyes, her mouth opening slowly. Whatever she had been expecting to hear, it wasn't that.

"My life?" She asked. She meant for it to come off

incredulous, but all she could hear in the tone was fear. She cursed herself for not keeping a better hold on her emotions.

Priestess Reed stared down at her with disdain, her lip curling slightly.

"Yes, Miss Johnson." She spoke as if this should have been obvious. LJ wished there had been Becoming Ceremony preparation classes, something that would have warned of what was to come. "The good of the coven must come before the good of the individual."

LJ's stomach turned as the meaning of the words washed over her. Her parents never told her this was what she had to promise. They knew she didn't believe in the values of the coven, yet they had pushed her to do the ceremony regardless. They should have known she wouldn't do it. That she couldn't do it.

"Miss Johnson," Priestess Reed said in a stronger voice. LJ's eyes focused on her again. "Do you swear your life to the coven? Do you swear to put the needs of the coven before your own?"

Bile was rising in her throat. How could they ask this of her? How could they ask a sixteen-year-old to dedicate her whole life to this?

"No." The word was out before she had the chance to even think about it. Though her voice was barely audible, the word hung in the air between them.

"What was that?" The priestess's tone was hard and angry. LJ cringed back, years of training telling her that she didn't want to disappoint her. She took a deep breath. She couldn't do this.

LJ stood up and stared at the priestess in the eyes.

"Miss Johnson—"

"No. I don't swear my life to the coven." Her voice was calm and steady despite her shaky hands and pounding heart. *Don't let her see your fear. She will thrive on your fear.*

"Miss Johnson—"

Pride swelled in LJ's chest at the surprised and horrified look on Priestess Reed's face. The tables had turned. She had finally found a way to throw a priestess off her game.

High on this feeling, LJ grabbed the crystal ball that was sitting on the altar beside them and threw it to the ground. It shattered, throwing broken glass everywhere. For the first time that day, LJ was thankful for the thick gown covering her legs.

Priestess Reed gasped in a way that was perhaps more of an inaudible scream, her hand coming to her chest as she stared at the ground.

"Screw you and your coven," LJ said. "I want nothing to do with you."

She spun on her heel and stormed purposefully out of the small room. It gave way to a much larger room with many doors branching off of it, but she had her sights set on the largest set of doors right across. What was a walk quickly became a run as LJ left her life as she knew it behind, never once looking back.

THANK YOU FOR READING!

If you loved this book, I would appreciate if you would leave a review on Amazon, Goodreads, or anywhere else online. Reviews help authors more than you know!

Want more fun romance? Check out my other books!

ALSO BY ISABEL HANSEN
Scarlet Sun
Amber Stars
Witches in Love

So Much More *(Novella)*
Love Me Now *(Novella)*
A Corner of My Heart *(Novella)*
Come to Stay: A Holiday Novella Collection

ABOUT THE AUTHOR

Isabel Hansen is an emerging Canadian romance author. She is an asexual lesbian, and an LGBTQIA+ advocate. When she is not writing, Isabel likes to read and play with her two dogs.

If you'd like to get notifications of new releases and special offers on her books, join her email list or visit her website.

CONNECT WITH ME ON SOCIAL MEDIA

Website: isabelhansen.com
Instagram: @IsabelHansen_Author
Goodreads: Isabel Hansen *(Goodreads Author)*
Amazon: Isabel Hansen *(Author)*
BookBub: Isabel Hansen *(Author)*